# STRANGE MURMURINGS

By
Brent McGregor

**DUAL CROWS PRESS**
Sydney, Australia
MMXXV

DUAL CROWS PRESS
*Spinning tales of terror and make-believe.*
Sydney, Australia
MMXXV

This is a work of fiction. Names, characters, places, and incidents either are the product of the author's imagination or are used fictitiously. Any resemblance to actual persons, living or dead, events, or locales is entirely coincidental.

ISBN 978-1-7643139-0-2



Cover design by LimeSpringStudio.com

For Amy and Roxanne.

Books by Brent McGregor

1.  Blood Tide
2.  Strange Murmurings
3.  Denizens of Darkhaven

# Contents

# Author's Preface

Like a lot of writers, I fit my writing into the cracks of everyday life—between a full-time job, family, and other commitments. The stories in this collection were written over the past several years, in those precious snatches of creative time.

Together, they form a kind of sampler—offering a glimpse into my style, and (I hope) a few satisfying chills for fellow fans of supernatural horror.

I'm also thrilled to say that my debut novel, *Blood Tide*, is out now! If you enjoy this collection, I'd love for you to check that out as well.

You can sign up for my newsletter at www.brentmcgregor.com to get updates on future projects, behind-the-scenes bits, and the occasional ramble about books, horror, and writing life.

Thanks so much for picking up *Strange Murmurings: Short Stories*. I hope you enjoy the read. If you have a moment to leave a review—or even just a rating—on Amazon or Goodreads, it would mean the world.

— Brent McGregor, September 2025.

# The Hum

The fluorescent light hummed overhead, its insipid glare made the woman appear old and sallow. Oda Fosset routinely visited the practice for a range of bogus maladies, which were, more often than not, simple bouts of hay fever.

"Allergies again, Oda?" I said, shuffling the papers on my desk.

"Don't poke fun, George. I might be getting old but I'm not senile."

I fidgeted.

She waggled a wrinkled finger in her ear as if cleaning out wax. "I keep hearing this God-awful hum. And it worried me, so I got Clara to drive me right over."

She lived with her fifty-something spinster daughter, Clara, and despite Oda being completely overbearing the majority of the time, the two of them were inseparable and could be seen driving about town in Oda's '75 Lincoln Continental just about every other day.

"When did this start?" I held back a yawn.

"Last night. I thought it was the fridge at first. Just this real low drone."

I took the auriscope from my desk drawer and examined her ears. "Have you experienced any blockages?"

"No," she said, playing with the thread of her cardigan sleeve.

"And how about your glands, are your glands up?" I felt under her neck for tell-tale signs of swelling.

"What do you think, George?"

"Could be tinnitus," I said, sitting back down. "It tends to get worse with advancing years. Have you had your hearing checked lately?"

She shook her head.


Marty Tidwell was a rough chicken farmer from out at Dilith Creek who had a reputation as the town drunk. He had been experiencing a burning sensation, and had, what we call in the medical profession, a mild case of the clap. I got through prescribing him a course of antibiotics and telling him to lay off the drink when he too complained of hearing a hum.

"I tell you what it reminds me of Doc," he said. "It's like that white noise you hear when you're trying to dial-in the right radio station."

"When did you first hear it?" I asked, checking his ears as I'd done for Oda.

"When I was out cleaning the sheds yesterday morning."

"And you don't remember hearing any loud noises recently that could have affected your hearing?"

He shook his head.

I frowned. I checked his blood pressure, but everything appeared normal.

"And you can hear it now?" I asked.

He nodded.

"It's the darndest thing, Doc. It's like I'm on the wrong frequency, or something, stuck between the channels."

I didn't know what to make of it. I mean, two patients in one day, with different ailments, both with the same set of unusual auditory symptoms? It was peculiar. Such a coincidence would arouse the suspicion of even the most complacent of doctors.

"Oops. Sorry, George," said Peggy, taking her headphones out.

She was a good receptionist but often missed hearing me on the office intercom.

"You can go in now, Sheriff," she said.

The man in the waiting area stood up. Sheriff Raban looked like a linebacker with paddles for hands. He wore his off duty plain clothes and had his yellow Labrador, Bessie, with him.

"I don't know, George, this hum, it's awful loud," he said in my office a short time later. "It's a constant pulsing… like the sound of a faraway diesel engine. What if I'm going deaf?"

Bessie lay by her master's feet, resting her head on her paws.

I formed my fingertips into a steeple. "Let's not get ahead of ourselves."

The sheriff had been receiving treatment for a stomach ulcer and not his hearing, two conditions generally considered as mutually exclusive.

"But what if, I don't know, I have a brain tumor, or epilepsy, or something?"

I sighed. "You won't have any of those things, Sheriff."

"Are you sure?"

"Trust me," I said, leaning back in my swivel chair. "When you hear hoofbeats, you've gotta think horses, *not zebras*. The best diagnosis is often the simplest."

The sheriff harrumphed.

"Bessie agrees with me, don't you, Bess?"

The dog looked at me and wagged her tail.

***

A warm breeze rolled in from the desert, kicking up dust as it went. I shielded my eyes. Fumbling with my keys, I did a last-minute inspection before locking up.

"Night, George!"

Peggy waved from the passenger side of a Nissan Skyline. I smiled and waved.

I liked Peggy. She was smart, funny, and generally dependable. Behind the wheel, her boyfriend, Todd, gave me a reverse nod as they rolled past.

They edged out then disappeared up Main Street.

The road and adjoining car park were all but empty, and the surrounding buildings, diffused with shadow, had turned sepia in the softening glow.

Something brushed against my leg and I heard a familiar purring.

"Hey there, buddy," I said.

Smokey was a long-haired stray that had started coming around weeks earlier, and I'd gotten it into my head that I might try and tame him.

"I was wondering when you were going to show," I said, taking a tin of sardines from my pocket.

Smokey blinked his yellow dish plate eyes and licked his lips.

I knelt, peeling back the pull-tab and setting the tin down for him.

He ate with alacrity.

"Same time tomorrow then?" I said, leaving him to his banquet.

I hopped in my pickup and headed for home.

The darkened stores along Main Street appeared vacant and cold, however, the neon sign of the tavern shone bright, and the streetlights blinked on as if to signal my passing.

The welcome sign on the outskirts of town got me thinking of my ex-wife. We had moved from Santa Fe six years previous, for the change of pace and the sense of community. But, living in San Alma wasn't what it cracked up to be. It was different from city living. San Alma is a small town, remote, isolated. There's no *Starbucks, McDonalds*, or even a *Taco Bell*. There's no movie cinema or shopping mall. It's quiet. If it weren't for the occasional tourist taking the wrong exit off the highway the town wouldn't get any visitors at all.

I was tired, thinking about dinner, and was reaching into the glove box for a breath mint when a convoy of trucks shot past, overtaking me on my right. They were *hauling ass* as well as freight, stirring up billows of dust as they went. Where's the emergency, I remember thinking.

Switching on the radio, I dialed into the nearest station.

*"Silver wings shining in the sunlight..."*

Merle Haggard sang over the airwaves.

I let myself be hypnotized by the broken centerline and the sound of the tires on the tarmac. It's beautiful out there at night. The town is bounded by the imposing Sierra Malvado Mountains. It's desert country — which means big skies, and stars, lots and lots of stars.

*"Don't leave me I cried, don't take that airplane ride."* continued Merle.

That's when I saw it.

I thought it was a rain cloud at first, moving and shifting on the horizon, but as I got closer I realized it was a giant flock of birds. Hundreds if not thousands of birds. The sky was thick with them, flying overhead in a whirling ever-changing pattern, a great dark mass of wings and feathers.

I held the pickup steady, arching my neck, trying to steal glances from under the visor.

Odd. It was like they'd all been stirred up. They flew this way and that. I'd heard of starlings behaving like that before but never many species of birds like that together. They swooped so low at one point I thought I might hit them with my pickup.

Distracted I hadn't realized I'd drifted across the center lane line, and nearly blinded by the headlights of an oncoming vehicle, I swore, swinging the wheel violently, careening onto the hard shoulder by the verge, fishtailing on the gravel before coming to a stop.

White knuckled and still gripping the wheel, I let my head sink forward onto the back of my palm. I applied the emergency brake. My heart was pounding.

I opened the door and slid out of the driver's seat, nearly stumbling when my boots touched gravel.

The birds still wheeled overhead, babbling and cawing. Back aways the other vehicle had also swerved to a stop. The driver got out.

"Are you okay?" I called out.

He gave me the thumbs up.

I pointed up at the mass of birds.

He nodded and then shrugged.

We stood and watched for a while, in wary silence, before eventually the birds dispersed, we got back in our vehicles, and parted ways.

***

Several uneventful weeks later, when I'd settled into

the daily routine, and the incident with the birds had faded into the background of my memory, I was on my way to work, and stopping at the stop sign on the corner of Marques and Webber, window down, marveling at the rays of sunlight appearing golden above the mantle of green in the park, a car came hurtling into the intersection.

Traveling well over the speed limit, the car wavered uncontrollably, before applying its brakes and screeching to a stop. A cyclist, who had been leisurely pedaling past moments before, just narrowly avoided being flattened by swerving up the sidewalk into a nearby hedge.

The driver honked their horn irritably.

I recognized the car, a '75 Lincoln. Is that Oda Fosset?

"Are you kidding me lady!" yelled the cyclist, after extracting himself from the hedge, his legs and arms covered in a profusion of tiny scratches.

The driver's side window wound down, proving my assumption correct.

What the crap? That is Oda, I thought.

She swore at the cyclist, flipping him the finger before she sped away.

Some shopkeepers had gathered on the sidewalk and muttered amongst themselves. The poor cyclist was left dumbfounded and ashen-faced. I spent the rest of the car ride puzzling through what happened.

Strangely there were a handful of patients already waiting when I arrived to open up. The telephone rang as I was inviting them in. Unbeknownst to me, Peggy was already sat at reception.

"San Alma Medical Centre," she said, in her over-rehearsed telephone voice.

I nodded hello, before getting the patients to sit.

"Uh-huh. Well, I'm sorry to hear that," Peggy continued on the phone. "Well, I don't think we have any timeslots left for this afternoon," she said, her fingertips tapping out a clickety-clack tune on the computer keyboard. "Doctor Callan is very busy. But we should have a spot tomorrow?"

CLICK.

Peggy shrugged and put the handset down on the cradle.

"Good morning, George," she said, sounding out of breath. "Sorry about that. I guess he must have hung-up."

The telephone rang again, but I stopped her before she could answer this time.

"What's going on?"

"It's been like this all morning," she said, "The phone hasn't stopped since I got in."

I frowned.

"It's weird, they all say they can hear a strange humming."

I felt a sinking in the pit of my stomach and my muscles tensed.

I couldn't dismiss this as mere coincidence. How was it that so many could now hear the hum? How was it that so many were affected? Was this some kind of collective hysteria, or was I standing at ground zero for something more sinister?

"I'll be in my office," I said flatly.

"George, there's something else too," she said, wringing her hands.

"Yes? What is it?"

"Todd, my boyfriend, can hear it too."

***

When I closed up that afternoon I heard raised voices coming from the direction of the car park. Edging closer to investigate, I saw Peggy and Todd standing next to the same Nissan Skyline from the previous evening. They were arguing. She was upset, shaking her head. It was impossible to tell for sure but she might have been crying too.

Todd, all of a sudden, cried out like he was in pain and doubled over covering his ears.

Peggy put a hand on his shoulder, but he straightened up, grabbing hold of her wrist.

"Hey!" I yelled, taking a step forward.

They froze like deer in the headlights.

Todd gave me a level stare, while Peggy broke free of his grip. I would have done more except she gave me a surreptitious signal to stop, mouthing the word *don't*. Todd then escorted her to the passenger side of the vehicle, and they drove off.

What was with today? Everyone seems on edge, I remember thinking.

I went back to lock-up and that's when I heard this godawful yowling. Ears turned back, tail twitching left and right, Smokey slunk out of the shadows.

"Hello you," I said, tin of sardines at the ready. "Where have you been?"

Smokey paused. He looked wild-eyed, different, and his fur was dirty and matted.

"I know what you want," I said, setting the tin down.

His movements were skittish. He padded forward slowly.

I knelt to stroke his back, but, hissing and growling, he reared back and took a swipe at me.

"Gah!" I yelled, feeling the sting of the feline's claws.

I swore, and Smokey bolted back to the safety of the shadows.

"Yeah, you better run!" I called out after him.

I checked the back of my hand finding a pair of red parallel lines.

"Great. Just great," I said going back inside to clean and dress the cuts.

Tiny plumes of red blended with the water as it disappeared down the drain. Serves you right for trusting a stray, I thought, washing my hand under the tap in my office. Still, before tonight, I thought I was winning him over.

Then I got to thinking about Peggy and Todd, arguing like a couple of strays in the car park. Strange. I made sure to apply some antibiotic cream before putting on a bandage, as I'd seen cat scratches turn septic before.

The neon sign of the tavern down the street seemed to beckon, and all at once, I needed a drink. Inside, the tavern was dimly lit. I sat down at one of the wooden barstools, and the barkeeper got me a brew. The place, empty except for a handful of patrons, smelt of fusty carpet and stale beer. I fidgeted absentmindedly with the label on my beer bottle, studying the lines of liquor all lit up along the shelves behind the bar.

"Howdy Doc," said a slurred voice, as they sat down beside me.

I recognized Marty Tidwell's weather-worn face.

"What brings you to a classy establishment such as this?" he said, making a sweeping regal gesture.

I tilted my glass.

He nodded. "Tough day?"

"You could say that," I said.

"I've had a pretty tough day myself" — he gulped his beer — "well…couple of days."

He fussed and pulled at his ear.

"Are you still hearing it?"

He gave me a blank look, took something from his left and right ear, and set them on the counter, taking his hand away to reveal a pair of cotton wool earplugs.

"It's all I fucking hear, Doc. Heck I'm hearing it right now."

"Are you serious, Marty? Why didn't you come see me?"

"I tried. This morning I rang to get an appointment, but you were too busy."

He said these last words using his fingers as air quotes.

"Well, we've been under pressure with an overwhelming number of patients and calls. But I'll make time. You come see me tomorrow okay?"

"Alright, Doc," he said taking another gulp of beer.

I smiled a relaxed smile.

"What happened to your hand?" he said, motioning to my bandage.

"What? Oh that," I said, setting my beer down. "Cat scratched me."

He raised an eyebrow. "I didn't pin you as a cat person."

"I'm not," I said. "Not usually." And I told him about Smokey, and about how he'd been hanging around the practice. "But the thing is he's never attacked me before."

Tidwell chortled.

"What's so funny?"

"Nothing. I just had a thought is all."

"What? Tell me," I said, and took a sip of beer.

"It's just…I guess we've both had some *bad pussy* lately hey, Doc?" he said (a crude reference to his gonorrhea), breaking into hysterical laughter, slapping me on the back.

Some beer went down the wrong way: I coughed and spluttered.

When he finally did stop laughing, he went all quiet, and said, "You say this cat never tried to scratch you before?"

I shook my head.

He rubbed his beard stubble.

"What?" I said, adjusting the bandage on my hand.

"Nothing."

"No really, what?" I pressed again. "Tell me."

He sighed. "Well first there's this humming noise, and people are hearing it, me included, then all sorts of animals around town, like this cat of yours, have been acting strangely."

"What do you mean 'acting strangely'?"

"I don't know…like hostile, agitated."

"Agitated?" I rubbed the back of my neck.

"Yeah, like scratching people for example."

I frowned.

"First Travis Powell gets knocked down and trampled by his own cows. And then my chickens get all bloodied from the constant feather pecking. I tell you something weird is going on."

I sipped my beer. "And you think the hum has something to do with it?"

He nodded. "Lately coyotes have wandered into town like they ain't afraid of nuthin, and dogs are scared, so scared they piss themselves."

"Well come to think of it I had a pretty weird experience myself the other night." I told him all about the incident with the birds and my near miss on the road.

"There! You see. Someth—

"Aaah!" screamed Marty, his face contorting into a mask of pain. He doubled over covering his ears.

"Wh-what's the matter?"

Everyone turned, blinking, looking bewildered.

"Jesus Christ. Can't you hear that?! Are you all deaf!" he said, attempting to snatch up his earplugs, succeeding only in brushing them onto the floor. "Oh, God, it's getting louder!"

"Are you okay?" I said, putting a hand on his back.

"Get your hands off me!" he cried, knocking me back.

The barkeeper motioned like he was getting ready to do something, but, Marty picked up his glass, and flung it at the wall behind the bar, causing several bottles to shatter in an explosion of glass and liquor.

Everyone looked at Marty with a mix of pity and astonishment.

He looked around in desperation, before loping out of the bar, and into the night.

***

There was a spate of new cases, starting the next day. Patient after patient came to me, claiming they could hear it, scared, tormented, troubled by a strange relentless hum. The phenomena oddly appeared localized only to San Alma. Although lacking all the hallmarks of a virus, it spread with the same ruthless efficiency. Existing patients, added insomnia, headaches, and anxiety to their growing list of symptoms, their condition seeming to worsen. It was becoming increasingly clear we had a problem in San Alma, and when the media got hold of it, even the occasional tourists stayed away.

The mayor petitioned the government to have an official investigation conducted, and sure enough, several weeks later, some high-profile researchers — with all their sophisticated equipment and tracking devices — came down from Santa Fe to detect and locate the source of the so-called San Alma Hum. A town meeting was called where they could report their findings.

"Good evening, ladies and gentlemen. Thank you all for coming," began the man at the lectern.

Someone cleared their throat. A baby cried. The air was fragrant with the musty smell of disuse, and sour percolating coffee. We sat in rows of stackable plastic chairs. I picked out some faces from the crowd. Sheriff Raban gave me a nod from across the aisle. Oda and Clara Fosset were there too, as were Peggy and Todd. It seemed like the whole town was present.

"My name is Philip Kaufman. I'm a scientist. I'm a doctor in biochemistry, as well as a university lecturer," he continued.

Kaufman was a tall, officious looking man, with thinning gray hair, and an equally gray suit. He wore a pair of oversized metal-framed glasses, with thick lenses, which gave him the bulging-eyed appearance of a praying mantas.

"I lead a team of researchers," said Kaufman, gesturing to several impassive looking men sat behind him. "I would like to start by thanking the mayor for inviting us to speak here today on this matter.

The presentation went on for about twenty minutes, various slides, graphs, and scientific terms were used.

"After much deliberation," he concluded, "it is our professional and expert opinion that there is *no* discernable source, no evidence, of any *mysterious* low-frequency hum."

There came an angry murmur from the gathering.

"And so without further ado," he said, looking about the room, "we will open the floor to any questions."

A wave of anger coursed through me, and, feeling compelled to speak, I sprang up and said, "You say there's no evidence of the hum, but how do you account for the many hundreds of San Alma residents who've presented themselves at my Practice over the past couple of months, complaining of hearing the noise?"

There was a murmur of agreement from the assemblage.

Kaufman seeming nonplussed said, "I'm glad you asked, Doctor…?"

"Callan," I said coolly.

Kaufman nodded. "Doctor Callan…we're not refuting at all that people *think* they hear this sound. We are simply saying there is no scientific evidence to support its existence outside of each individual hearer."

I raised an eyebrow, waiting for him to continue.

"In other words, we suspect this phenomenon can be put down to either some very active imaginations or a type of collective mass hysteria."

"With all due respect," said a familiar voice from the crowd.

It was Oda Fosset.

"With all due respect Mister Kaufman," she said, a waver in her voice, slowly standing, "I think you're all a pack of liars!"

There was a breathless gasp from the gathering. And although it was far away, I could still discern the twitch of Kaufman's jaw muscle.

"What about Roswell?!" said an angry voice from the back of the hall.

"What?" Kaufman said, taken-a-back.

It was Tidwell.

"Roswell. It's close by isn't it?"

At this point the mayor stepped up to the lectern, allowing Kaufman to sit.

"Only serious questions please," said the mayor adjusting his tie, "I think we can all arrive at some plausible answers without having to resort to any tinfoil hat explanations."

"I'm serious," yelled Tidwell. "What if it's the military, testing some kind of top-secret weapon. Have you investigated that?"

"I think that's enough questions for today," said the mayor turning off the microphone.

"I'm telling you they've got something in that mountain!" yelled Tidwell.

***

Shortly after, the scene descended into a free-for-all

of angry shouting, and petty infighting. I retreated out a set of double-doors at the back, bursting out into the cool night, doors slamming behind me. I stood for a moment, leaned up against the handrail of the entranceway steps, grateful for the fresh air.

A few, like me, must've left early, and were milling around by the water fountain.

That's when I heard a loud — *Slap!* — followed by the sound of a sobbing.

Even from across the square I recognized Peggy. She took a couple of backward steps, clutching her cheek. Written on her face was an expression of astonishment and betrayal. She was with Todd who was raging and hurling abuse. He slapped her again, this time grabbing her by the shoulders, shaking her like a ragdoll.

"Stop!" I yelled and started running. No man, as far as I was concerned, had any right to raise a hand to a woman and I wasn't going to stand for it. I bolted across the uneven ground.

Peggy tried to fight back, but then, before I could cover the full distance, he hit her again, hard, with his closed fist. She went limp and fell to the ground unconscious.

I swore and launched a punch at Todd, but he must have seen it coming, because, quick as lightning, he did a side step collecting me in the middle with a solid left hook, knocking the wind right out of me. He screamed and before I knew it he had his hands around my neck, choking me.

"Todd…" I gasped, struggling for breath trying to prize his fingers loose.

He had the eyes of a madman. I hit back but it didn't faze him. A black cloud spun into my field of vision. If I don't do something soon I'm going to blackout, I thought.

I reached into my pocket and, brandishing my keys like a set of knuckledusters, drove them, as hard as I could, into his face. He let me go and I dropped to my knees, coughing and spluttering.

He staggered back, clutching his face.

Screaming in outrage, he lunged at me again.

Bang!

A gunshot.

We froze in place.

Sheriff Raban stood aiming his gun. "Alright Todd, knock that shit off. I don't care who your old man is!"

Todd glowered. I noticed a trickle of blood running from his ears.

Some deputies turned up on the scene, no doubt drawn by the sound of the gunshot, cuffed him, and led him away.

The sheriff holstered his weapon.

"You okay?" he asked, helping me up.

"I've felt better," I said, rubbing at my neck.

"Peggy!" I said, rushing to check on her. She groaned. I folded my jacket and put it under her head.

"She'll have a real shiner in the morning," said the sheriff. "What set him off?"

I shrugged.

"It's unlike Todd to behave like that. I know his mother. The boy's a kitten," he said.

I then told him how I'd seen them arguing in the car park at work several weeks earlier, and how Peggy had said Todd was now hearing the hum. And I told him how I had seen blood running from Todd's ears.

The sheriff wrinkled his brow.

"What are you going to do with him?" I asked.

"Well, he's going to spend some time down at county," he said. "You really did a number on him."

"I did a number on him?" I exclaimed.

The sheriff chuckled.

"Hey, I've been meaning to see you about my hearing problem anyway."

"Are you still hearing it?"

"Yes, I'm still hearing it," he said sharply. "I've lost my appetite. Bessie's been acting weird. I can't sleep. I mean if it's not the hum keeping me awake it's all those damn trucks."

"Trucks? What trucks?"

"Oh, just these bastard big rigs, semis, y'know? They keep driving past my place in the middle of the night. And I tell you, George, there ain't nothing out there. It's nowhere near the highway, so what the heck are they doing there?"

***

Ring, Ring.

The incoming call light on my desk phone lit up, flashing red like some emergency beacon. I sighed, pinching the spot above the bridge of my nose. I'd given Peggy time off, and given my current mood, I didn't feel like speaking to anyone.

"Hello?"

I was surprised to hear sobbing at the other end.

"Doctor?" said a woman's voice.

"Yes. Hello. Who is this?"

"Clara," said the voice, in barely a whisper.

I had to think for a moment, flicking through my mental Rolodex. "Clara Fosset?"

There came more sobbing at the other end, before her abrupt reply.

"Mom's d—dead."

I tensed. There was a horrible heavy sinking in my stomach.

"Oda? Dead? Are you sure?" I said, in a shaky voice. Oda might have *imagined* she was in failing health, but she had been in good health really considering her age. "You need to hang up and call 911."

"Mom had you on speed dial. You were the only person I could think of to call. She's dead, George. I'm sure of it. I tried CPR, but it's too late! She's not breathing."

"Clara, calm down. Tell me what's happened."

"She was in the g-garage," she said, bawling. "At first I thought there was fire — because of all the smoke."

She broke down into more heart-rending sobs.

"It's okay, Clara. Tell me," I said.

"I was coughing, so I opened the roller door, to let out all the smoke, and that's when I noticed the car's engine was still running…"

The poor woman let out a sound that was halfway between a moan and a whimper.

"You can get through this," I said.

She took a breath and said, "Th-there was a hose…from the exhaust to the driver's side window. At first, I thought she was sleeping Doctor, but — oh my God—"

I winced.

"I tried to wake her, but she was already dead. She was already dead!"

The receiver trembled in my hand, as I listened to the anguished cries of that poor woman. Why would Oda have taken her own life? It didn't make sense. She was an eccentric, sure, but she hadn't seemed suicidal. At least that had been my impression.

She loved that Lincoln, I thought, but in the end, it was the old girl's death trap. Perhaps in her mind, it was the closest thing to taking it with her.

I took a pained breath and closed my eyes. I felt partly responsible. She had been my patient, and as a doctor didn't I have a duty of care? Had I failed to read the signs?

Stop it, I thought, tightening my grip on the receiver. Thinking like this does no one any good.

I managed to calm Clara down, reassured her as best I could that it would all be okay, and expressed my most heartfelt sympathies, before hanging up. I then went round directly to announce it.

***

Days later I received another phone call. This time from the Shady Pines Hospital out at Los Alamos. They rang to tell me Marty Tidwell was in the ICU.

The poor boozehound had gotten hammered and hacked off his ears with rusty garden shears.

He had lost a lot of blood by the time the paramedics had got to him, they said.

And most bizarrely of all — he had been smiling, muttering something about having found a way, a way to switch radio frequencies.

***

When the sheriff skipped an appointment I naturally became worried. Something was up. And so, I closed up The Practice early, to pay the man a house visit.

As I was leaving, though, I found Smokey's pathetic crumpled form on the step. He was stiff and cold, affected by mange, it wasn't clear what he'd died of. Hunger most probably. I felt numb, guilty. I picked him up and placed him, temporarily, in a cardboard box I found in the alley.

I just got in my pickup and drove.

Sheriff Raban lived in a farmhouse on the edge of town. I had to take the old scenic road, lined with sagebrush and dotted with potholes. It was late afternoon by the time I got there, and the shadows had grown long. The mountains stretched out before me like the devil's backbone. I saw birds flocking again, far off on the horizon. The sky was filled with them, a black swirling mass of ill portent.

I turned off the road onto the sheriff's property, after recognizing the familiar faded sign, the tires of my pickup kicking up dust and gravel.

All seemed still at the farmhouse. When no one came out to greet me, I simply pulled up behind the sheriff's flatbed. I figured he was home since it was parked in the usual spot.

Just another house visit, I thought, stepping up onto the front porch. I froze. The door was ajar. Lots of townsfolk were in the habit of leaving their doors unlocked, I tried to reassure myself, but still, my skin crawled.

I gently eased the door open and called out "Sheriff? It's me, George Callan. I came to see if you're okay?"

I waited. There was no reply.

I pushed the door all the way open, stepping inside. The living room was dark and noticeably cooler than outside. A ray of light beamed through the window, however, illuminating a cloud of dust. I heard the ticking of the clock on the mantle. The place was in disarray. Furniture was overturned. Books and sundry items were strewn all over the floor.

"Sheriff?" I called again, making my way into the quiet shadows. The floorboards creaked under my shifting weight.

I stopped at the base of the stairs. "Hello?" I called out, looking up in the direction of the bedrooms.

Nothing. An oscillating electric fan hummed on the sideboard.

I started up the stairs, but stopped when I heard movement from the back of the house.

Now, you work hard and long enough hours as a doctor, and you'll get to see, or experience, some pretty unsettling things. Disturbing things. I was a Peace Corps volunteer for a while. You get to face down sickness, death, and suffering on a regular basis. So, what do you do? You just sort of switch off. You have to. But, as it turns out, I still wasn't prepared.

In the kitchen, I found the sheriff slumped in a chair. He had committed suicide with his own pistol — decorating the ceiling with his brains.

I was shocked. It took me a moment to grasp what I was seeing.

Something crunched beneath my boot and I realized the floor was littered with broken glass, various boxes, and foodstuffs.

And then I heard a low guttural growling.

My blood went cold.

I turned and saw Bessie, bearing down on me, snarling and frothing at the mouth. I lunged for the table in an effort to grab the gun but the dog was too fast. She latched onto my ankle, her fangs sinking deep, ripping and tearing.

I cried out. The pain was excruciating. I lunged for the table again, this time snatching the gun from under the dead man's hand. I fired off two shots, shooting Bessie dead.

I checked my ankle. It was all tore up to hell and covered in blood. I first looked at the sheriff, then at Bessie, and then back to the sheriff again. Feeling faint I sank into one of the kitchen chairs.

The windows of the house rattled. I looked out and saw the dark shapes of the birds flocking. Had they followed me? I heard their twittering and cawing. My mouth felt dry and I tried to swallow. Are those lights? I thought, getting up.

I was fascinated to see a line of headlights, a convoy of trucks, slowly snaking their way up the mountain. What are they doing there? I thought.

A dark shape, probably a crow, suddenly flung itself at the window, making a sickly thud. The windowpane exploded in a cobweb of broken glass.

Then, I hear it, a pulsing whirring vibration in my ears. Terrible. Faint at first but getting louder. The sound of it is so piercing, deafening, it shakes the foundations. I cover my ears. I cannot think. It's getting louder. So loud that I might go mad from the pain. The hum!

# Until Midnight

"You still here?"

Edward looked up from his work cubicle to see one of the firm's co-founders smiling down at him, a veteran lawyer in a Brioni suit.

"Fraid so, Mister Weiss."

Stretched out behind them was an impressive panoramic view of the New York City skyline at night. They were alone, except for the janitor, who started up with the vacuuming.

"I know we're paying you, Edward, but…don't you have somewhere else to be? It's New Year's Eve."

"I've got to finish drafting this contract."

"Well, don't overdo it. There is such a thing as burnout. You should hit the bars. Cut loose, y'know," he said, putting on his overcoat and gloves.

"When I was a first-year law associate, I was at a party every night."

"Is that your professional legal advice, sir?"

Weiss laughed. "You bet. Happy New Year, kid," he said, making a beeline for the elevators.

***

Some hours later, Edward stood in the elevator, loosened his tie, then yawned, watching the arm of the ancient semi-circular floor indicator descend through the levels: 27, 26, 25, etc. At the 23rd floor, the elevator slowed, then stopped, the doors opening with a characteristic 'ding,' and he met eyes with *the most beautiful* young woman he'd ever seen.

She was exquisite, with pale, almost luminescent, skin, sandy blonde hair, and haunting blue eyes, a startling hue, enhanced by the cornflower blue of her outdated dress.

She smiled at him demurely, before stepping in.

With an armful of work files, she struggled to reach the buttons of the floor selection panel.

"What floor?" asked Edward.

"Thirteen," she said, in a lilting voice.

Edward paused. *Had there always been a Level 13?* He couldn't remember. He'd always assumed the building's architects had omitted the number, for time-honored reasons of superstition. But there was the button.

He pressed it, and the elevator started up again.

He cleared his throat. "Burning the midnight oil?"

"Sorry, what — Oh, shoot!" she said, losing hold of the work files, which scattered across the elevator floor. She knelt to pick them up.

"Let me help you with that," he said, helping gather up the papers. "You work for *Ventralux*?"

"How did you —"

"It's on the letterhead," he said, handing back the papers.

"Right…of course."

"Y'know, I've not been working here long, I don't think —"

"We make soap and laundry detergent."

"How did you know what I was going to ask?"

"Everyone always does," she said, and shrugged.

"I'm with *Simpson and Weiss*."

She gave him a blank look.

"The law firm on 28."

An awkward moment passed.

"We deal with commercial law, finance and banking, taxation, that sort of thing. Which, I guess, saying it out loud…sounds less interesting."

"Less interesting than soap?" she said.

They laughed.

The elevator slowed, then stopped, the doors opened, and this time a short skeevy man stepped in. He had dark slicked-back hair, and wore a sweater jacket, over a white shirt and tie.

"What's buzzin, Jane?" said the skeevy man. "You stayin' for the bash?"

"I already have plans," she said.

"Plans? Don't be a square," said the man. "Stay. Plans are meant to be broken."

"Can't," she said.

"Aww c'mon now. The sales boys have already cracked the champagne. You could bring your boyfriend here," he said, motioning to Edward.

Edward looked first at Jane, then at the man, and back at Jane again. "Oh, we're not—"

The man guffawed.

"You'll have to forgive Frank," she said, shooting the man a dagger-eyed look. "He has a bad case of *foot in mouth*."

Again, the elevator slowed; this time Edward felt a pressure build-up in his ears before they went pop, a sensation that always reminded him of scuba diving. The lights flickered then the doors slid open, to reveal the 13th floor. The sound of merrymaking and chatter filtered in.

"What's your name, friend?" asked Frank, holding the elevator door open.

"Edward."

"Okay, Eddie. You coming?"

Edward looked at Jane, who smiled a reassuring smile.

"C'mon," said Frank. "Join us. Don't be a party pooper."

* * *

The thirteenth floor was open plan, arranged into rows of desks and filing cabinets, with venetian blinds on the windows, and a large philodendron plant in the corner. Colorful pink and white streamers, with matching balloons, adorned the room. The words *Happy New Year* were spelled out, in bright and colorful bunting on the wall.

Oddly, there were *no* computers. None. Only typewriters. And beside each typewriter was an old-fashioned black bakelite rotary dial telephone.

Stranger still was the way people were dressed. Groups of partygoers milled around, chatting and laughing, laughing and chatting. The men wore sack suits, or cardigan and tie combinations, whereas, the women wore pencil skirts, with pillbox hats, or hats with veiled fascinators.

Edward's head throbbed and there was a ringing in his ears.

"Okay, I'll bite. Is this fancydress or something?" he said, looking around. *This is all too real*, he thought. *This level of detail can't be faked.* Looking back at the elevator, he wondered if he'd stumbled into some kind of *Back to the Future*, or Narnia-type situation. He pictured himself being interviewed on TV for the daily news: just another krank with a tall story.

Somewhere, through some speakers, played the "da-da da-da rock" of old-school drums and guitar.

"What's that Daddy-o?" asked Frank.

"Is this, like, a film set or something?" said Edward.

Frank lit up a cigarette.

"What do you mean?" said Jane.

He was about to say something, when some partygoers jostled past, blasting party blowers and whirring noisemakers; they too were dressed in outdated clothing. *I'm definitely not in Kansas anymore*, he thought.

Frank took another drag of his cigarette, and looked at Edward quizzically, before exhaling a long trail of smoke. "Hey, bean. You okay? You're lookin' a mite green."

"Never mind," said Edward, rubbing the back of his neck. *I'm dreaming,* he thought. *That's it, I've hit my head, and I'm hallucinating, and any moment I'm going to wake up.*

"Listen," said Jane, gently touching his arm. "I've got to drop these files off, but I'll be back, okay?"

Edward nodded.

"Can you show him around, Frank?" she asked.

"Sure-thing, toots."

And she sashayed off in the direction of the corner office, disappearing behind a petition of frosted glass.

Frank whistled. "I hate to see her go, but I love to watch her leave."

Edward couldn't help but agree.

"C'mon," said Frank, and they crossed the floor, to where a man with a loud voice stood regaling a group of clingers-on.

"So, what are we talking about?" asked Frank.

"The Russians," said the loud man.

He was a tall burly man, with an Orson Welles-style beard.

"What about em?" said Frank, reaching into an ice bucket, retrieving a couple of beers. He popped the tops off and gave one to Edward.

"They've just put a satellite in space."

Edward scratched his head. *Is this a prank?* he thought. *Are they pranking me? Because it doesn't feel like a prank. This feels real.*

"Where did you hear that?" asked Frank, and took a swig of beer.

"From Howard."

"Howard? What a schmuck," said Frank, using a nearby waste-bin to ash his cigarette.

"He read it in *Times Magazine*. It's up there circling the globe now, as we speak. What d'ya think of that?"

Frank ashed his cigarette again. "Well, you shouldn't believe everything you read."

The loud man scoffed. But then, noticing Edward, stuck out his hand. "Sorry, I don't believe we've met."

"This is Eddie," Frank interjected. "He's with Jane."

Karl raised an eyebrow. "Sooo, which part of the apple you from, Eddie?"

"Brooklyn."

"Brooklyn huh? I don't usually get there myself. The wife, and I, just found this unreal apartment here in Manhattan." Turning to Frank he said, "Guess how much?"

Frank shrugged.

Karl whispered the answer into Frank's ear, as if it were a big secret.

"Phh! Your mother," said Frank, looking indignant.

"Yeah, I know." Karl grinned.

"I remember when the subway used to cost a nickel," said Frank, shaking his head.

"So, did you watch the Yankees game on the weekend?" asked Karl.

"I'm more of a *Mets* fan," said Edward.

At that moment, Jane came back, and, linking her arm with Edward's, said "Mind if I steal him for a bit, boys?"

"I thought you couldn't stay?" said Frank.

"Well, you know…broken plans and all that," said Jane.

"Swell. Just swell," said Frank, smugly. "Steal away then."

As Jane led Edward away a few steps, he heard Karl ask, "Who are the Mets?"

***

"I thought I'd come rescue you," said Jane, when they were out of earshot.

"Well, it's nice to be rescued," said Edward, grinning.

"Drink?" she offered, seeing he had finished with his beer.

"Sure," he said, and they walked over to a trestle table, which, set out as a buffet, had an abundance of dishes, all strategically placed: hotdogs, hamburgers, a quivering jello mold, what looked like banana cream pie, and a big ol bowl of spiced pineapple rum punch.

She poured them both some punch, and his heart skipped a beat when her hand lightly touched his.

She was a vision. Her pale waxlike skin made her look like a doll, and her blue eyes, of the brightest azure, seemed to have an inner glow all of their own.

"So, what do you do, when you're not lawyering?" she asked.

"I go to the gym, and…I like to run."

"Running? Isn't that a lonely pastime?" she said, letting the cup's edge linger on her bottom lip, for just a moment.

He cleared his throat. "I like it. Predawn. The fresh air. The chance to be alone with your thoughts. How bout you? Have you worked at Ventralux long?"

She sighed. "Yes, a long-time. Sometimes it feels like forever."

"I know the feeling," he said — even though he didn't. He'd worked for *Simpson & Weiss* for about a nanosecond, and before that, a string of part-time jobs. He found himself trying to impress her. He took a sip of punch. She was lovely, but she had an ethereal quality, a sort of unspoken sadness, which he couldn't quite pinpoint.

"Hiya, Jane!"

Edward turned to see a woman with bouffant hair, and horn-rimmed glasses, approaching. She held a glass of red in one hand, and a cigarette holder in the other.

"Aren't you going to introduce me?" said the woman.

"You're right. Where are my manners?" said Jane. "Edward, this is Val, from accounts — she's the one who put this little soiree together. Val from accounts, this Edward."

"Hello," said Val, then took a sip of wine. "So, where did you find this one, Jane?"

"In an elevator."

Val smirked. "Maybe I should ride the elevator more often. Do you like the party so far, Edward? Are you having a good time?"

"Aha, sure," he said.

"And, do you plan on staying?" asked Val. "Will you join us for the countdown?"

Jane looked up expectantly.

"I don't know. Maybe. New Years isn't usually my scene."

"Not your scene?" said Val.

"Really?" said Jane.

He shrugged. "I don't know. New Years always felt kind of sad to me, empty somehow, like a pantomime: the fireworks, confetti, and everyone wearing those funny paper hats."

"Oh, fudge," said Val, spilling wine on herself, "I'm such a klutz. Excuse me, you two," she muttered, and wandered off.

"Is that really how you feel about New Years?" Jane asked.

"Huh?" said Edward, distracted, by the wall clock and how late it was getting.

"New Years…Is that really how you feel?"

"Well, kind of."

"I don't know how anyone could not like New Years," she said, and then, almost by rote, "A moment in time; the convergence of old, and new; the commencement of a new year. The promise of a new beginning."

"That's nice. Who said that?"

"I just did, silly," she said, and giggled.

"Well, I like it."

"Have you made any new year's resolutions?" she asked.

"Me? No. I already quit smoking."

"But, you've got to have goals right? I mean…what do you want out of life? Put it this way — if you only had one day left to live, how would you spend it?

"Hmmm," he said, rubbing his chin. "I suppose I'd call that pretty girl I just met, and ask her on a date."

Jane laughed. "You're cute," she said, maintaining eye contact with him. "Sounds like you've got it all worked out."

He smiled. "How would you feel about me kissing you right now?"

She tilted her head slightly. "But, it's not even midnight."

He leaned in, and running his fingers through her hair, he kissed her. She cooed. Her lips, although lovely and soft, were, oddly, without moisture; a thought he dismissed nearly as soon as it occurred to him.

"Stay," she said, blushing, taking his hand. "Until midnight."

***

Jane led Edward back to where the others were gathered, the revelry, by that point, was in full swing, lively, if not debauched: a couple of the sales guys were fighting and throwing champagne; someone vomited in a wine cooler; and Frank eagerly drank champagne from a woman's shoe.

"What have *you two* been up to?" said Frank, suspiciously, wiping champagne from his chin.

"Nothing," said Jane, shrugging.

"Is *nothing* code for necking by the punchbowl?" he asked, then laughed.

Jane shot him a look.

"You gonna join us, Eddie? You stayin' for the countdown?"

Edward glanced at the clock again. It was almost midnight.

"Sure he is," she said, taking Edward's hand again. But this time, he flinched. *Her hand is cold, almost icy*, he thought.

Everyone began the countdown. "TEN, NINE..." they all shouted in unison.

He looked at her hand in his, and he was baffled: her skin, once so luminescent, now appeared wan, and gray.

"EIGHT, SEVEN..."

*Is that smoke?* he wondered.

He thought back to moments before, to when they'd kissed. *How welcoming her lips had been. But then, there had been something not quite right about them, hadn't there?*

*It looks like smoke.*

"SIX, FIVE..."

*It had been their apparent lack of moisture. Her lips were dry and sort of — what?*

"FOUR, THREE…"

Jane put a hand to his cheek and kissed him, and, without quite knowing why, he shivered. It was as if someone had walked over his grave.

*Lifeless. That's what her kiss had been.*

TWO, ONE. *HAPPY NEW YEAR!"* yelled everyone, cheerfully, throwing bunches of streamers, and confetti, blowing or whirring their noisemakers.

*It even smelled like smoke now.*

Edward gasped, removing his hand from Jane's, backing away.

A rousing chorus of *Auld Lang Syne* started up.

"Wh-what's wrong, Edward?" said Jane advancing, her facial expression changing. Her eyes grew wide, and her mouth went slack. Her skin became even more gray, sallow.

He was the first to see the orange and red flame as it leaped from the waist-paper-bin, and up the wall, moving vertically as well as horizontally, igniting the furnishings and party decorations.

It was miraculous how quickly it spread.

The partygoers, having realized their predicament too late, screamed, searching in vain for exits. Their way was blocked, blocked by the fire, a crackling, growling, beast, whose hour had come at last. Black smoke pooled on the ceiling. Fire engulfed everything, from the rows of desks to the files and streamers. Balloons popped. The large philodendron simply combusted from the heat. The once bright colorful bunting, that spelled out *Happy New Year* upon the wall, curled up and turned to ash.

There was a flash, an explosion of glass, and Edward was thrown backward.

All about him, people burned, glowing roman candles, lit by the light of their own suffering. Their skin shrank, and limbs contorted: blackened skeletons, grim marionettes without strings.

Consumed by flame, one of the figures stumbled forward, grabbing Edward by the collar, its death-like grip burning holes in his jacket.

Edward screamed. *How is it still alive*, he thought.

"Eddie," it cried, the words coming out all strangled.

It was Frank, his features melted.

"Fuck! Fuck. Fuck," said Edward, breaking free of its grip, frantically patting out the flames on his jacket.

It laughed maniacally. "You party pooper."

A blistered and charred phantasm, glided, almost floated, towards him. It was Jane. The flesh had peeled from her once beautiful face, revealing a set of skeleton-like teeth; her expression warped into a grimace, her eyes empty glowing sockets.

"Kissss meeee Edward," it said.

He screamed, jumping backward.

"You have to stay, Edward," it pleaded. "For me…Please. Forever."

At that moment, he felt a flash of heat and searing pain as a mote of flame shot up his leg. *Escape*, he thought. *I have to escape.* And, in a panic, and hardly able to breathe for all the smoke, he dashed the windows. But they, being the floor-to-ceiling type, were well sealed. Coughing, suffocating, he beat his fist on the glass, but to no avail; it just would not break. He picked up a nearby office chair and threw it. The glass shattered.

Cold air rushed in from outside, feeding the flames. He recoiled from the heat, unable to breathe. He leaned out, squinting through the haze, at the darkness down below. Smoke poured up and out. It was a long way up, and he felt light-headed. *My God, there's no fire escape.* he thought. *Where's the fucking fire escape?!*

He looked around for another way out, anyway, at all. But there was only the fire. *Oh, God,* he thought. *It's either the quick way down or, a long and painful drawn-out death.*

*There's nothing for it but to jump.* He swallowed, and closing his eyes, he leaned out, then took the plunge, toppling end over end into the dark of night.

***

A sea of darkness revolved. Edward awoke. He blinked once, then twice, slowly, raising his eyelids until they were all the way open. The first thing he was immediately aware of, was the pain in his arms and legs. *Are they broken?* he thought. He was dizzy, and his head hurt like a son of a bitch.

"There he is," said a familiar voice.

"Mister Weiss?" said Edward. And, realizing he was in bed, in a state of semi-undress, tried to sit up. It took a lot of effort.

"I was wondering when you were going to wake up. Don't exert yourself, kid. Just you lie back and rest."

He winced and lay back down again.

"Where am I?" asked Edward, looking around, dazed. He saw the IV drip and the bedside monitors.

"Bellevue Hospital," said Weiss. "You took quite a nasty fall. I came by as soon as I heard. Your mother's gone to fetch the Doctor."

"What happened? How did I — Did they put out the fire?"

"Fire? What fire?"

"In the building," said Edward.

Weiss looked at him with an expression somewhere between amusement and pity. "There wasn't any fire, Edward. The paramedics found you last night, unconscious, battered, on the staircase of the twelfth-floor fire escape."

Edward threw off the blanket and was shocked to find his legs done up in plaster casts — but apparently unburned.

"What's going on? I saw the fire. There was a fire. I saw it with my own eyes. I felt it. And, what about all those people?"

"What people?" said Weiss, looking even more confused.

"At the party," said Edward.

"Party?"

"Ventralux. Level 13," said Edward.

Weiss gave him a peculiar look. "Ventralux?" he said, in surprise. "I've not heard that name in ages. And there's not been a Level 13 in the building, since before the refurbishment. Who put you up to this? Is this some kind of publicity stunt? Because, honestly, I think it's in poor taste."

"Wh-what do you mean?" said Edward.

"Ventralux," said Weiss.

Edward store at him blankly,

"The tragedy," said Weiss, as if he expected Edward to know what he was talking about. "I mean, sure there was a fire, but in '57...65 years ago. All those poor souls, lost. The poor bastards...the architects left out the fire escapes."

# The Eye of Anunreshka

Those first few weeks after the disciplinary hearing were painful, to say the least. I avoided friends, family, and people in general. I needed space to collect my thoughts, to prioritize, to get my life back in order. It was a Tuesday, and I'd not spoken to anyone for days. That's when I heard from Lane.

Professor Lane was a heavyset man, with prematurely white hair. A doctor of psychology, he was also one of the leading Parapsychologists in the country.

We sat in my kitchen drinking coffee.

He adjusted his glasses. "How's my star protégé?"

I laughed. "Star protégé? I wasn't aware I was so well regarded by the staff at UVA."

"You do yourself an injustice, Max. Your lectures were always well received. They were wrong to dismiss you. I hope you know I fought the decision."

"I'm sure you did everything you could."

There was an awkward silence.

"Is Trish here?" he said, looking around. His eyes scanned the counter beside the sink, where, weeks earlier, I'd started a collection of empty beer bottles.

I shook my head. "She's at her mother's."

He looked at me with that same patronizingly sympathetic look I'd seen from so many others. "How are you doing?"

"Well, you know…I take each day as it comes." I shrugged. "Anyway, to what do I owe the pleasure of this visit, Professor? I doubt this is a social call."

"Astute as always." He smiled. "Okay, I'll get down to brass tacks. Do you remember Adera Moseley, from your time at the university?"

My memory conjured up the image of a beautiful young woman, lying next to me, vulnerable and pale, on the bedsheets of a Motel 6.

I nodded.

"She's a gifted student," he continued, "and I have reason to believe she is a Psychic. She's the real deal, Max."

"I know," I said. I thought back to all those student experiments with the colorful Zener cards.

She'd received top marks, surprising everyone with the speed and accuracy in which she guessed the symbols.

"And you'll remember me having mentioned the Poynter House in my lectures, no doubt?"

"Sure. Number one on *Waggoner's List of Virginia's Most Haunted Houses*. I believe *you* called it your 'white whale.' But, what does one have to do with the other?"

"Some days ago, Adera came to me saying she'd had a lucid dream. About an old house by a river. A house she felt drawn to."

"Let me guess. The Poynter House?"

"The very same. I made the connection right away of course, but we were also able to match it using this." He slid a photo across the table.

I picked it up and examined it. "But isn't the Poynter House off-limits?"

"That's what I thought, too. It was tied up in legal red tape for years: contests over possession of the estate. I made enquiries, and it turns out the Poynter House has new owners. A conglomerate based out of Florida. And they've got a half-baked idea of turning the place into a themed hotel. They think there's money to be had: their target market being the sickos and morbidly curious."

"I remember a certain University Professor being morbidly curious himself, back in the day."

"Yes…jokes aside though, we've been permitted to go in and investigate."

"Who is *we* in this scenario?"

"I'm putting together a team of paranormal researchers. There's me of course, Adera, young Charlie Webber from the camera club. We'll need to document everything. And there's you, Max. I hoped you might come along."

"You're not serious?"

"I am. We could use your expertise."

"What's in it for me?"

"I will personally see to it you are reinstated to the faculty at UVA."

"I don't know," I said, rubbing the back of my neck.

"It wasn't my idea, y'know. It was Adera's."

"Adera's?" I exclaimed.

"'He has to be there,' she said. You were in her dream, Max."

***

The Poynter House was situated on the elaborate grounds of the Carlisle Estate, about sixty miles from Richmond. Samuel Poynter, a wealthy industrialist, had purchased the 745 acres with his wife, Rachel, when they had moved from Massachusetts, with their son, in 1868.

All along the drive there I peered out the van window at the cold silent waters of the James River.

The van was loaded with specialist equipment. Charlie was at the wheel. I rode shotgun, while Adera and Lane were in the back. Lane wore his noise-cancelling headphones.

"Is he still listening to Wagner?" I asked.

Charlie smacked on chewing gum, and with his free hand, walked a coin across his knuckles. He grinned impishly when he got it right. "Uh-huh. He loves that classical shit. Gets him in the zone, he says."

Adera sat quietly, staring out the window. She'd not spoken more than two words to me since the start of the trip, but she now said abruptly, "There's going to be a lunar eclipse. A blood moon."

"A coincidence?" I asked.

"Nope," Charlie interjected. "The Professor said, 'In Eastern culture when the celestial bodies' — yadda, yadda, yadda — he said it would add to the ambience."

"What a night to visit haunted houses," I said.

"Yep," said Charlie.

We motored up the driveway, covered with debris and vines. The Poynter House loomed in the distance, beckoning. I shivered involuntarily. *Getaway*, my instincts said, *you're not welcome here*. I couldn't shake the feeling. Designed by Poynter himself, the house's architecture was all vaguely asymmetrical. It had a disorientating effect. Its sandstone walls were interlaced with dark grey stone, and every gable, every fascia, every board and trim, cast a shadow. Its boarded-up windows were lifeless eyes, watching.

The site itself, at one time, must have belonged to the Algonquin people, who were known to practice sharmanic rituals—a thought which made me uneasy.

After unloading the van, we climbed the front steps to the ornately carved oaken doors. Lane turned a key in the ancient lock; the doors swung open with an ominous creak. A rush of dank air escaped and a musty smell of decades' old decay assailed our nostrils.

We found ourselves in a spacious foyer, complete with a large central staircase and elaborate wooden panel work. Judging from the dust and cobwebs, no-one had set foot in the house for years.

***

By the time Charlie and I finished setting up the camera equipment and motion sensors in each of the rooms, Adera had wandered off. I searched, and a short while later found her standing in the sitting room, gazing at a portrait above the mantle. Her opalescent green eyes were glassy, entranced. I couldn't help thinking how beautiful she was, in her inimitable way: mysterious, with long cascading raven hair.

"It's Rachel Poynter," she said, referring to the subject of the painting.

"Uh-huh," I said, still looking at her.

She shifted her gaze to the next portrait of: a man, neatly dressed and carrying a walking stick. He had a sullen aspect.

"And that's Samuel Poynter — or 'The Beast,' as people called him." She coughed, then took an inhaler from her pocket and used it. "He murdered her y'know."

"So I've read. She and their little boy, right?"

She nodded. "Nobody knew why. But, tonight we could find out."

I looked at the paintings.

A moment passed.

Her eyes met mine. "Max, I'm sorry…y'know…about what happened."

"It's fine. Trish was going to find out eventually. Things worked out for the best."

She looked down, wringing her hands. "I'm glad you're here."

I smiled. "I wouldn't have missed it."

*** 

Lane had us set up the bulk of the equipment in the foyer, the most well-lit room in the house. We had floodlights running on battery packs, and moonlight shone through the stained glass window above the entrance, bathing the foyer in a rose-colored glow.

All books on the subject of the paranormal attach importance to the hour of midnight; generations past called it "the witching hour," a time when, supposedly, otherworldly things happened. But midnight came and went without incident, so I assumed the night was a bust, when —

Charlie stood up. "What the — "

"What?" said Lane.

Charlie pointed. "One of the sensors…the temp's dropped."

"Where's that?" I said, as we gathered around the monitor in question.

He pointed to a section of the floor in front of us.

Adera strode forward, closing her eyes. "Definitely a cold spot," she said, feeling the air with her palms. She coughed, readying her inhaler. There was a cold gust of air. We heard the piping sound of a child's laughter. It came from upstairs at first, but then it echoed everywhere.

Adera stepped back behind the line of cameras and monitors.

"Tell me you're hearing that," said Lane.

Then we saw it…

A swirling mist-like shape materialized, hovering for a moment before morphing into the spectral figure of a boy.

Charlie swore under his breath.

The air was electric. It gave me gooseflesh. I couldn't believe my eyes. It was there, but at the same time wasn't.

Adera took a hit on her inhaler and grabbed my hand.

"What's it doing?" whispered Charlie.

Lane shushed him.

It sat at the base of the stairs, rocking back and forward, oblivious to our presence. It was looking down at the carpet by its feet. Again we heard the echo of child-like laughter.

It turned and faced us, its unblinking pupil-less eyes all dark and lifeless, its mouth opening and closing in silent colloquy.

"It's trying to communicate," said Lane, stepping forward.

It froze, its mouth opening wide, its face transforming into a hideous gaping death mask. There was another blast of air, followed by an ear-shattering scream.

Then…nothing. It vanished.

"Where'd it go?" said Charlie.

We heard the same childlike laughter again, followed by the sound of invisible footfalls on the stairs.

"C-mon! Bring the cameras," said Lane, in hot pursuit. But his legs went out from under him, and all his considerable weight and years came crashing down. He fell onto one knee and went sliding across the floor.

It had come and gone as quickly as it had first appeared. We heard nothing but the sound of Lane's moans: the sad and inconsolable sound of someone who had had their dreams dashed at the last moment.

"What happened?" said Adera, rushing over to help. "Are you injured?"

"It's nothing," said Lane, who tried to stand but collapsed back down.

"This must've been what tripped the Professor," said Charlie. He held it to the light for closer inspection. "What is it?"

I squinted. "It's a marble."

Charlie scratched his head.

I laughed. "Didn't you ever play marbles as a kid?"

"No." He rolled his eyes. "I had a PlayStation," he said and pocketed the marble.

Lane groaned.

Charlie retrieved a walking stick from a selection in an oversized vase. "Here," he said, handing it to Lane. The head of the stick was capped with the silver impression of a scowling dog's face. It looked like a museum piece.

"Well, that was exciting," said Lane, using the walking stick to stand. He limped over to the monitors. "Never in my wildest did I expect to see an *actual* full-body apparition. Please tell me we got that on tape."

We played back the video, frame-by-frame, but to no avail. We saw ourselves in the foreground, keystone cops in some silent movie. But there was no shadowy figure, no blurry apparition. The thing was invisible.

The audio recordings, however, were a different matter. I imagine if any professional cynic had heard what we heard, they would have simply called it auditory pareidolia. But we heard it nevertheless, a child's voice, faint but discernible, barely above a whisper. "Beware the eye of Anunreshka."

***

Naturally, we were excited. We'd witnessed the truth about life after death. We'd made contact with a non-corporeal being. It seemed like our ghost-hunting venture had paid off. However, despite having seen the thing with our own eyes, our physical evidence, was inconclusive. Lane feared the EVP recording would be dismissed as a flight of fancy. And so, we all agreed to stay on, in case there were any new developments.

"It sounds like it's saying Anunreshka," said Charlie. "What do you think it means?"

I shrugged. "A place name maybe?"

Adera stood up. "Do you hear that?"

"Hear what?" said Charlie.

"A woman's voice," she said, walking away.

Lane began to get up but I stopped him. "I'll go," I said, grabbing a flashlight.

I found Adera in the drawing-room, again staring at the portrait of Rachel Poynter. I'd seen the same unwavering look in her eye before, during the countless hours of ESP experiments back at the University.

"Sensing something?" I asked.

The candelabra on the mantle ignited all on its own, brightening the immediate space.

I swallowed. "Weird."

She nodded. "Where's Charlie with his camera when you need him?"

"I'll go get him."

"No, not yet," she said, touching my arm.

And, as if on cue, the portrait first tilted then spun on its nail a full 360 degrees.

"Woah!" I said, stepping back.

"Look," she said.

The portrait depicted Rachel Poynter in a red gown, with flowing ebony hair. She was beautiful, but she had the kind of smile one might show the world to try and hide their sadness.

"Do you see her hand?" Adera said. "It's pointing over there."

We walked briskly to the adjacent room, which, turned out to be the library. It was filled with relics of olde-worlde furniture, covered in yellowed drop sheets and cobwebs. I shone my flashlight on the shelves, inspecting the faded spines of all the neatly arranged volumes.

"Like astronomy much, Poynter," I said under my breath.

"What?" said Adera.

I took some books down for a closer look. "It turns out that Poynter was reading books of the occult: *The Ars Goetia, the Picatrix,* the *Kitab al-Azif.* I mean…this isn't normal bedtime reading."

She frowned.

While I returned the books to their former position, something toppled down.

"Wait. What's that?" she said.

It was a small leather-bound notebook.

Adera opened it and read the first few lines.

"This is her journal. Rachel's journal. She meant for us to find it."

*February 2, 1868*
*It has only been a few weeks since we moved into the new house, here on the Carlisle estate. I feel blessed. Samuel is a clever husband. He designed this grand house himself, and I am so looking forward to the years ahead. I love him.*

*I confess, though, that I already miss our old cosy townhouse. The house here is perhaps too large for our needs. The rooms are cold and draughty. It is winter after all and we are close to the river, the harsh winds blow in from the Atlantic, and sweep across the grounds of the estate.*

*Samuel is often away on business, and so I frequently find myself at a loose end, alone in this house, except for our son, and the servants. I have started this journal, which I will write in whenever I feel inclined.*

*Mother says she will visit in the spring. I am so longing to see her, so we can talk together freely. For, as brilliant a conversationalist as Samuel can be, he has been inclined to moodiness of late. He is a mercurial man.*

*April 12, 1868*
*I am in constant astonishment at the grandeur of this*

*house and its sprawling rooms. We would have been just as well suited with a little cottage. It will take time for me to adjust to life here. Nevertheless, it is starting to feel more like home.*

*I have to find new ways to entertain myself. The help keep much to themselves, except for Ainsley, the groundskeeper, who brought us fresh fruit and vegetables from the markets today. I was touched by the young man's kindness.*

*Samuel makes regular trips into town, but he is working too hard, and when he is not working he spends hours alone reading the books in his study. He has developed a keen interest in astronomy. He has also developed the curious habit of taking solitary walks of an evening. I often wonder what he does there in the woods at night. When I ask him, he changes the subject.*

*From the upstairs window, I have seen him walking the banks of the river, walking a strange and shuffling step. His behavior is beginning to worry me. He seems less and less interested in the upkeep of the house or in the maintenance of the business. It might be my imagination, but, one particular night as I saw him returning from the woods, the wind blew in such a way that I think I heard the faint sound of chanting or singing.*

*Stranger still, Mother wrote to me and told me of a letter Samuel had written her asking her to delay her visit, citing reasons of business as an excuse. I burst into tears upon reading this. I can scarcely imagine why he would have done such a thing.*

*July 26, 1868*

*I am anxious. Samuel has been too engrossed in his studies and research. I am worried about him. He is spiraling into longer and longer bouts of depression. His hair is uncombed, his cheeks are unshaven, and he has somehow acquired a limp (necessitating the use of a walking stick, which he now carries with him everywhere). He has taken to sleeping in the library. Last night I saw him arguing with Ainsley. I hope it wasn't over anything serious.*

*September 5, 1868*

*A police officer by the name of Cartwright came to visit the house yesterday. He was looking for Ainsley. Apparently, the young groundskeeper has not been seen for days, and his mother reported him missing.*

*It isn't like Ainsley to go off without telling his mom, Cartwright had said. Ainsley has a reputation for being reliable, and is not at all prone to drink or to play at cards etc.*

*Samuel spoke with Cartwright at length, offering to help in whatever way possible, saying he would be in touch if Ainsley ever presented himself.*

*Earlier tonight, though, I observed Samuel, again from the upstairs window, entering the woods on one of his regular evening walks. I have never known him to behave so secretively. He was carrying a hessian bag and kept glancing from side to side. His behavior so unsettled me that I stepped back from the window to conceal myself, lest he glance back in my direction.*

*October 14, 1868*
*Cartwright came to the house again today, this time warning us to keep our doors safely locked. He implied there might be a gang of undesirables about.*

*They had found Ainsley in the woods, he said, with his eyes gouged, his heart excised, and his body impaled on the sharpened bough of a birch tree.'*

*I am terrified and dismayed. Who would do such a barbarous thing? It makes me sick to my stomach.*

*March 21, 1869*
*May the saints preserve me. For tonight, while walking past the closed door of Samuel's study, I heard the most unnatural of sounds: deep and guttural voices mixed with an unholy sigh or gasp. I knocked on the door but Samuel did not answer. That is when the chanting began...*

*'Hear my plea, Oh Lord of Vision. I speak with your lips. I breathe with your breath. I see with your eye. I beseech thee. Iä! Anunreshka! Iä! Anunreshka! The immortal...'*

*On and on he went like that for many minutes.*

*I found the whole incident most disturbing. Later, when I asked him about it, he simply shot me an intense stare and told me to mind my own business. I am afraid, and I never thought I would be afraid of my husband.*

*May 8, 1869*

*I didn't know what else to do. Samuel had changed, the servants had all left us, and there were a series of nights demarked by chanting and ghastly sounds. Therefore, I resolved to break into Samuel's study to see the extent of evil that he hid from us.*

*I waited until he fell asleep, and took his key.*

*The room reeked due to the heady mix of incense that still hung in the air. I was taken aback. There was a circle, about nine feet in diameter, with an intricate pictogram scrawled in chalk upon the floor, with a malevolent looking eye symbol at its center. Half melted candles lined the walls. I searched the room. Samuel evidently had been preoccupied with various books and tomes: some written in German or Latin, and another in Greek.*

*In the center of the pictogram lay a hessian bag. I picked it up to examine further, but quickly dropped it again when I realized it contained what looked like the bloody remains of a human heart. I fled from the room, trying not to be sick, and was careful to lock the door—making sure to return the key to its hiding place.*

*P.S. I suspect that Samuel now knows I'd entered the room. He looks at me differently. Later, when I asked him about poor Ainsley, he looked at me most peculiarly indeed.*

*June 5, 1869*

*I never thought my son and I would be captive in our own home. I have now barricaded us in the master bedroom. I believe Samuel means to kill us.*

*Cartwright visited this evening under the pretense of asking Samuel for his advice about a business venture. But it soon became evident that the man's real intention was to ask Samuel about his part in Ainsley's murder.*

*Voices were raised. There was an altercation and—my God—Samuel knocked the man unconscious, setting him alight with lamp oil. The poor soul must have been in absolute agony, writhing and twisting on the floor, screaming in that high-pitched inhuman scream. He died terribly. I can still hear his screams.*

*I don't know what to do.*

*Samuel has lost his wits completely. His whole bearing has changed. I can hear him chanting and singing in the study even now as I write this.*

*I hear taunting voices outside the window at night. I feel as though we are being watched, as if the walls have eyes—and there is a thumping and crashing as if there were something in the walls*

This is where the entries stopped.

I exchanged a glance with Adera. The diary explained everything.

Charlie burst into the room. "Come quick. Something's wrong with the Professor."

Returning to the foyer, we found Lane slumped in his chair, surrounded by camera equipment and cables, still gripping the head of his walking stick. Pale and sweating, he had removed his jacket and tie. He was muttering.

"Are you okay, Professor? Is it your knee?"

"Oh, M-Max, what is it?" He had a vacant look in his eye.

Charlie frowned. "I gave him aspirin."

I decided not to tell Lane about the journal, not wanting to excite him.

The silence was broken by a staccato electronic beeping.

Charlie stepped away to check one of his gadgets, which had lit up like a Christmas tree, blinking with so many red and green lights. "One of the infrared sensors—picking up movement in the upstairs hallway. The night feed should catch it."

On the monitors, however, we saw nothing but an empty hallway. I could have been fooled into thinking I was looking at a frozen screen if it weren't for the occasional static flicker of the grayish-green image.

"It's Rachel and the child…and they're scared. Come on!" said Adera. She grabbed a flashlight and took off running.

"Wait," I said, but she was already halfway up the stairs, Charlie close behind, adjusting the lens on his shoulder cam as he went.

Lane stood to follow.

"You've gotta be joking," I said.

"I'm not going to pass this up, Max."

"Suit yourself."

The landing was cloaked in gloom. I shone my flashlight and caught a glimpse of Adera and Charlie moving rapidly down the hall. We were in hot pursuit, Lane's walking stick making a – thump, thump, thump – sound on the carpet, the many side rooms and doors a blur.

Adera froze beside the final door, putting a finger to her lips, gesturing for us to be silent. She reached for the handle. Charlie adjusted his lens. Lane was breathing heavily. My heart was beating fast. I felt a cold draft of air and heard the echo of a woman's weeping, following closely by the great whomping sound of invisible footsteps. We were pushed aside like playthings. The door opened then slammed.

"He's after her. It's him," said Adera, rattling the door handle.

"Who?" said Charlie.

"The Beast."

The latch gave and the door swung open. It was an expansive room, empty except for a four-poster bed. The door to the balcony was open, curtains fluttering in the night breeze. The gibbous moon cast dappled shadows on the mosaic patterned carpet.

"Narhh-aghgh!" Lane collapsed to the floor.

"Is he alright? Give him space," I said to Charlie.

I was about to kneel beside him when a swirling mist-like shape materialized, this time morphing into the shape of a woman, all white and semi-transparent in the moonlight.

Adera grabbed my arm. "It's Rachel," she said, with a hushed reverence.

She was dressed in clothes of the previous century, and in her arms, she held the ghost-child we had seen earlier. She wore an expression of such sadness.

I was torn between attending to my friend and observing this spectacle.

There was a flash of movement out of the corner of my eye, Charlie groaned, and I saw him fall to the floor.

Adera screamed.

Whirling around, I was surprised to see Lane somehow on his feet again, with walking stick raised menacingly, his face a mask of rage, his eyes filled with hatred. He brought it crashing onto my head. I toppled backwards and the world spun, a carousel of needles and stars.

Through the misty red veil of semi-consciousness, I saw Adera wrestling with Lane, trying to restrain him, but was tossed aside for her efforts. Charlie lay opposite, his unblinking eyes staring at me from his collapsed and bloodied face.

I tried to stand, but seeing stars again, slumped back down.

Lane's appearance seemed to change, his features warping until they looked like the sullen man from the portrait. I was amazed. The resemblance to Poynter was uncanny.

"Rrrgggggarr!" Lane lunged at the ghost woman.

She raised her hands to hold him off, and to defend the boy.

"Stop!" I cried.

He struck at them with that walking stick, that artefact of evil, again and again until they dissolved away into nothing but fragments of moonlight.

He stood there, hunched and jeering on the balcony, covered in Charlie's blood. And he began to chant, the words rhythmic and unrecognizable.

There was a trick of the light, and I realized the moon was in its final phase. The Earth's shadow crept across the surface of the moon until it had turned blood red.

The eclipse, I thought, and I tried to stand again.

The house shook, and the room began to shrink. I heard the clicking and clanking of something heavy, moving in the walls.

Lane looked first at me, then at Adera, and lifted back his head, letting out a peal of wicked laughter. His eyes rolled back revealing the whites of his eyeballs, before he collapsed, convulsing.

There came a sonorous eerie whistling, followed by a whirring, culminating in an almighty roar, so deafening I thought it might tear open the very fabric of reality.

I watched in horror as Lane's belly pitched and rolled under his shirt, as if something moved there, under the skin.

"Nooo!" cried Adera, springing forward. "I won't let you." She knelt beside him placing her palm over his stomach. "I won't let you use him!"

There was a flash; a shadow moved between them. Lane stopped convulsing and gasped for breath.

Finally, I managed to stand, and with my head pounding, I made wobbly steps towards the balcony. I almost tripped on the camera still lying next to poor Charlie's body. Invisible things whizzed and banged all about us, no doubt they were demons summoned by the baleful spirit of Samuel Poynter. The relentless blood moon bore down on us.

"Are you okay?" I asked Adera. But she didn't answer. She was in a trance.

Lane, on the other hand, had regained consciousness. "Max? What's going on?"

He was his old self once again and looked at me in bewilderment.

"My God, what have I done," he said, holding up his blood-specked hands. "What have I done!" He kicked the walking stick away, sending it skittering across the floor and under the bed.

"Adera!" I called, over the dreadful din as howling ghouls whizzed and flit about the room. "We have to get out of here!"

But she remained motionless, kneeling, head tilted forward, as though at prayer.

"Adera!" I called again, helping Lane to stand.

Her eyelids snapped open, and I was taken aback by the intensity of her stare, of her concentration. But there was something else too...Was it regret?

"I can't hold it," she said, shaking. "Go."

"We're not leaving you," I shouted.

"Go!" she screamed.

"Max!" yelled Lane, having regained his composure. "We've got to get out."

She mouthed the words I'm sorry, before coughing spasmodically. She fumbled, dropping her puffer before she could press it to her lips.

Her skin rippled as if there were something chord-like lashing about underneath.

She shuddered before letting out a godawful scream. Her body burst open like an overripe fruit, releasing a spray of crimson gore.

"No!" I screamed, in disbelief. She was gone.

I didn't have long to get my thoughts in order, however. I looked in horror, as something round and fleshy sprang from the blood and ichor in a wave of ever-expanding tentacles.

"Fuck this!" yelled Lane, grabbing my arm again. "Max, c'mon!"

And, quick as we could, we made our way into the hall; Lane with his arm over my shoulder, half hopping, half limping, the two of us like some demented three-legged sack race. All the while, we heard the crash bang of giant tentacled arms, reaching for us, trying to grab and latch.

We made it to the landing and I risked looking back. The thing, that evil cyclopean creature, was gaining on us, growing larger, barreling its way down the hall, knocking picture frames and plaster from the walls.

I don't know how we did it, but we bounded down the stairs, taking two steps at a time. But when we got to the base of the stairs, giant tentacles crashed through the outside wall. The colossal thing must have enveloped the entire house, I thought.

The stained-glass window burst inward in an explosion of glass, and an enormous three-lidded-eye, with a slitted dilating pupil, gazed down upon us. Within the eye lay a perceivable malign intelligence. In my mind, in a voice that was not my own, I heard the name Anunreshka, and I felt absolute unfathomable terror.

Narrowly being missed by a writhing tentacle, we dashed out the door and into the night air. The doors to the van weren't locked, and I jumped in the driver's seat as Lane piled into the passenger side.

"Shit." I searched the glove compartment and under the sun visor for the keys. "No. No. No." I realized, in our haste, we'd left the keys with Charlie's body back on the top floor of the house.

Out through the window, a collection of heaving tentacles reached in our direction.

"Here!" yelled Lane, fishing a spare key out of the van's ashtray.

I snatched it from him before turning the key in the ignition. The engine started on the first try and we sped along the drive, tires kicking up stones and dirt.

Reflected in the side mirror, I saw a great heaving mass of tentacles make a try for the van and miss.

We sped towards the main road. But, in the mirror, I saw the thing turn its attention back to the house, encircling it, clutching it like a greedy child. From within, the house glowed luminous red. There was a brilliant flash followed by an almighty explosion. A great tear in the fabric of reality opened, swallowing the creature and the house whole, imploding, contracting, sucking in everything around it in a matter of seconds.

I stepped on the gas. We skirted the James River, still awash with the sinister glow of the blood moon and we didn't slow down until we hit the interstate. I drove all night anxious to put as many miles between us and the Carlisle Estate as possible.

***

We were lucky to have survived. Lucky to have made it. But no amount of wishing would ever bring back Adera, or Charlie. Dead. Left behind. Taken. It was inexplicable.

I was filled with the full weight of my sadness. My grief was extreme.

We spent days on the road after that, moving from one town to the next, from motel to motel, for no other reason than we were afraid to go home.

Eventually, when we did go home, sure, the Charlottesville police had questions for us about what happened. The Daily Progress wrote up a story: Mystery Mansion Disappears, Baffles Locals. We told them a version of the truth, that is, the closest to the truth we could tell without guaranteeing us a one-way ticket to the loony bin.

Nothing ever came of it though. Charlie didn't have any family; and Adera's parents were far away in New York, so it got written up as a missing persons case.

I felt guilty about that one. I did. I should have told her folks about what happened.

Frequently now my nightmares take me back to that place, that night, and I see the three-lidded-eye of Anunreshka. I awake screaming.

# DreamSparkle

Well, don't stand there gaping you, idiot, get over here and help," Betty said.

Ned hustled to take the box from his wife. "Sorry, darling. Where do you want it?"

"Just put it with the others." She gestured to a stack of mover's boxes in the corner.

Betty shook out the tension in her wrists, surveying the mess that was the kitchen. *Oh God, it's hideous.* She hated everything about it, from the linoleum floor and laminate counters; to the avocado green splashbacks and yellow, patterned wallpaper. *What did I do in a past life to deserve this?*

She checked her cell phone in case there was a message from her tennis coach, anything to cheer her up.

"Look, I don't want to fight, okay?" Ned smoothed his tie. Dressed for work and with his wire frame glasses he bore more than a passing resemblance to Bill Gates.

Betty eyed his paunch. All through college—thanks to a lucky metabolism—he'd been lank and sinewy, but he'd packed on the pounds in recent years. "You always do this," she said. "I could have used your help cleaning and unpacking. You're not pitching in."

Ned winced. "It's not like I have a choice, darling. It's a new job."

Betty shook her head. It wasn't a new job, not really. Ned had been passed over for a promotion at the bank, then got himself transferred to a different branch—which was as good as a demotion in her eyes. They'd been forced to sell their beautiful apartment in town, trading it in for a postmodern fixer-upper in the suburbs.

She felt an all too familiar throbbing behind her eyes and pinched the bridge of her nose. It was probably a migraine. "Will you hurry? You've got to drop Alex at school, remember?"

"Oh jeez. Is that today?" Ned said, rubbing the back of his neck.

Their seven-year-old, Alex, sat at the breakfast nook eating Corn Flakes from an oversized bowl, watching them from beneath his shaggy fringe.

"Morning, kiddo." Ned ruffled the boy's hair. "You ready for your first day of school?"

"Not really," Alex said, munching.

"That's the spirit." Ned swiped a slice of toast.

"It's not my first day of school, Dad."

"We know that, chief," Ned said. "But it is your first day at a new school, and first impressions count." He ate the slice of toast before putting his jacket on. "You ready to go?"

Alex nodded.

On their way out, Ned leaned in to kiss his wife goodbye, but she shifted her head so he only managed to peck her cheek. He lingered for a moment before shuffling—with Alex in tow—in the direction of their lime-green Mazda parked in the driveway.

"Oh, Ned," Betty called out. "Did you contact the electricity company yet, to let them know we've moved?"

"Uh-huh. Yes, dear," he said, strapping Alex into the booster seat.

"What about Telstra?"

"The what?" Ned said, shutting the door on the passenger-side.

"The telephone company…to connect the phone?"

"Right—of course," he said putting palm to forehead. "I'll get right on it."

Betty watched them back out the driveway and disappear up the street.

***

A short while later, Betty slid an idle hand over the kitchen counter, appalled at the thin layer of grease she found there. It was filthy, a veritable history of food preparation. *No point in putting things away yet. This all needs cleaning.* And she slid the packing boxes into the living room—but not before shifting the ugly macramé lamp Ned's mother had bequeathed them a year earlier.

*What am I getting myself in for?*

While examining the sink—which was noxious-smelling, and covered with lime scale—she gave an involuntary shudder. 'There's more faecal bacteria in your sink than a flushed toilet,' she remembered hearing once. Still, she was surprised at the level of scum around the drain and in the crevices where the sink joined the counter.

The stove was an ancient-looking thing from General Electric, with a collection of knobs and dials more reminiscent, perhaps, of the Apollo 11 Space Module than a kitchen appliance. All its markings were worn-off, and the stovetop was foul with animal fat and cooking oil.

The bathroom, too, was a haven for all manner of putrescence. The toilet bowl was covered in grime and the bathtub had a dirty, brown halo.

She sighed deeply and put on rubber gloves. *Fuck my life. I hitched my wagon to the wrong horse.* She had loved Ned once, back when they were first married; he was laid-back, affable. But somewhere along the way they'd lost that spark.

Betty opened the fridge and cracked a cranberry wine cooler. It was early but this had never stopped her before. What was it that killed the spark, she wondered. The sex? Maybe. Ever since he'd gained the weight she wasn't attracted to him anymore. She'd feigned more than her fair share of headaches. *That isn't the real reason, though, is it? Nope.* She took a gulp of wine cooler. *You know what it is? He lacks motivation.*

Her mother was right. 'He'll never be successful,' she used to say. 'He'll never amount to anything.' It was true. Ned was supremely ungifted. Awkward. Ungainly.

She took another gulp of her wine cooler. He'd led them into one dumb financial decision after another, and that's why, now, they were living in this three-bedroom dive.

*Where did life go so wrong? I wasn't the most popular kid in high school but I wasn't unpopular.* She cursed under her breath. *I could have married Tim Dorsey from high school. He owns his own tech company. Probably owns his own Island, too.*

She sipped at her wine cooler, and thought of Jane, her girlfriend from book club. *Why couldn't I have married someone like Jane's husband, Andrew? He's an entrepreneur. He owns his own line of gas stations. He has a lucrative investment portfolio. I bet he doesn't drive a second-hand Mazda.*

She deserved better. She launched her empty at the bin. *That's why I don't feel guilty for sleeping around. Would Ned even care if he knew? Yes, but it wouldn't change anything. I'm not having my needs met. This thing with Mike, it isn't love or anything, just fucking. The truth is, before the affair, I felt kind of aimless, bored. Screwing Michael Foster—even if he is a better tennis coach than he is a lover—has made everything bearable. So, no, I don't feel guilty. Call it payback for allowing me to live in this squalor.*

While clearing under the sink, Betty moved a bundle of rags, which released a scuttle of silverfish. She squealed, squashing each of them.

After regaining her composure, she found, at the back of the cupboard, several dusty, piles of interior decorating magazines. They had titles like *Beautiful Homes,* and *Simply Vogue.* In addition, there was a box of something called DreamSparkle. "Lord, how long has this been here?" She said aloud, setting the box aside.

Flicking through several of the magazines, Betty thought that, perhaps, the previous owner had been one of these hoarder-types, seeing there were issues dating back decades. Turning the yellowed pages felt like stepping back in time. There were pictures of elegant dining rooms, stylish lounge rooms, luxurious bedrooms, and traditional kitchens. There was an abundance of furniture with fancy-sounding names: gainsboroughs, chesterfields, armoires, and chaise lounges. Indeed, as she thumbed the pages, she saw the fashions change from the bold abstract designs of the 50s and 60s; to the funky and psychedelic prints of the 70s; and the pastel colours of the 80s. Throughout were the usual series of display ads—for cosmetics, women's fashion, steak knives, and cleaning products.

One ad caught Betty's attention in particular, though, and that was an ad for DreamSparkle. Her eyes darted to her own box of the product before returning to the page. It was a full-page ad, showing an apron-adorned woman, standing in her kitchen, beaming a happy smile, a box of DreamSparkle in one hand, making a sort of voila-there-you-have-it gesture with the other. Betty raised an eyebrow. She flicked through the other magazines. *Strange, that the same ad should be in every issue.* It was the same ad, except the fashions of the woman, like the background, seemed to change through the years; from a pencil skirt with a bouffant hairstyle to blue jeans and a Farrah Fawcett do. You'd think they'd vary the ad a little, she thought. *That's just lazy advertising.*

She read the ad aloud, mimicking an infomercial-type voice. "DreamSparkle, Australia's number one disinfectant, and household grade cleaner, cleans bathroom and kitchen surfaces faster. Now with Forest Rain Scent." Again she eyed her own box of DreamSparkle.

"Worth a try I guess, " she said, shrugging and opening the box. She caught a whiff of forest flowers.

Following the directions on the back, she sprinkled the powder over the surface of the kitchen counter. Then, with a wet cloth, she rinsed. The mixture instantly fizzled, hissed, and bubbled.

"Oh wow! Is it supposed to do that?" she exclaimed, before turning the box over and reading the warning label:

*KEEP OUT OF REACH OF CHILDREN*
*AVOID CONTACT WITH SKIN*
*CALL 1-800-975-708*
*IMMEDIATELY FOR TREATMENT ADVICE*

"Good to know." She put the box down.

It was miraculous stuff, amazing, and it cleaned faster than other products.

First, she used DreamSparkle to clean the kitchen counters, wiping away the layers of grease and muck until they shone, immaculate. *How can I sustain myself in this loveless marriage? I feel like I'm in a vacuum without air. But I need to breathe. Do I still love, Ned? I don't know if I do.*

Then she moved to the kitchen sink. The mixture, again, fizzled, hissed, and bubbled. She scrubbed away the scum and grime, being careful to clean out the crevices where all those microorganisms could get trapped. *I've felt this way for a while. All this sneaking around. Avoiding getting caught. It makes me feel dirty.* She polished vigorously until the sink was brilliant and glowing.

Moving to the stove she used DreamSparkle to eliminate the copious food stains, soot, and food debris until everything was spick-and-span.

In the bathroom, she scrubbed the sink and toilet until they were both spotless and shiny-white. *I'm honest enough to admit I'm not happy. In fact, if I have to take one more night of Ned's awkward lovemaking I think I might scream.*

Betty used DreamSparkle on the bathtub, too, washing away the brown halo, erasing successive years of dirt and bacteria, until the tub was fresh and glowing. *I mean what's keeping me here? Not a lot, right? This shitty dive? A roof over our heads?*

*Maybe I should pack my bags and Alex and I can go live with Michael for a while. Michael's an idiot but I prefer his company to Ned's. In fact, I think*

*I will call Michael. Fuck it! I'll call him, now. I'll pack our bags tonight. Then, in time, maybe I'll file for divorce. Maybe even get my own little apartment in town.*

Betty pulled the tab on another wine cooler. It was already midday. She hiccupped. It always took her 'til her second or third to get a sufficient buzz going.

Returning to the kitchen, she stepped over the pile of magazines, setting the box of DreamSparkle on the counter. She removed her rubber gloves.

*Da-amn!* She looked around, tired, but impressed with her own handy work. *This place is looking cleaner. But hopefully, I won't have to stomach it too much longer.*

She took her cell phone from her pocket and started texting Michael—who was in her phone as Magic Mike.

*"Hey,"* she typed.

She waited. Three dots came up on the screen indicating that he was texting back.

*"Hey, yourself,"* he replied, adding the suggestive winky-face-emoji.

*"Can I crash at yours' tonight—I'll have Alex with me?"*

*"Sure. Is everything okay?"*

She started texting but her cell phone screen went black.

"Shit!" She threw her cell on the counter. What a time for the battery to go flat —and she had no idea which box the charger was in.

Tilting her head, she drained the last of her drink before discarding the empty.

She tried the landline phone next but didn't hear a dial tone. "Fucking, Ned," she hissed, slamming the phone on the cradle. "Still hasn't called the phone company."

*Screw it.* She made towards the fridge to get yet another wine cooler. Only, her foot slipped on one of the glossy magazine covers and she started to fall. Time seemed to move in slow motion. Had she been sober, she could have stopped herself—but she wasn't and didn't. She grasped at whatever she could, upsetting the box of DreamSparkle on the counter. She fell hard against the kitchen cabinets, then flat on the linoleum floor. Staring up at the ceiling light, she saw the box of DreamSparkle tilt and fall, releasing its corrosive, powder contents. There was a puff of white cloud and it was all over her, coating her face and chest, arms, and thighs.

"Oh, God! It burns! It burns!" she screamed, arms flailing. She closed her eyes then opened them. They stung like a son-of-a-bitch. Her vision blurred and the world was a kaleidoscope of smudgy shapes. She staggered to her feet, knocking over the macramé lamp.

*I'll wash it off.* She willed herself to the bathroom, where, she stripped to her underwear and jumped under the shower. The water didn't relieve the pain, though, or stop the burning. In fact, it made it worse. The water ran hard and the spray hurt horribly.

She was shocked when she looked at her own hands. They'd lost the upper layers of dermis and were pink and bloodied, emaciated, like something out of *Night of the Living Dead*. Between her feet, she saw the water mix with blood—and bits of what? To her horror, she realized they were pieces of her own skin. Her hands went to her arms and chest, and then to her face. She didn't recognize their features. Where they were once smooth and soft, they were, now, rough and textured. *My God, why is it still burning?*

"Oh no, no, no, no," she said, making a pathetic whimper-like sound.

*Is the whole world on fire?*

After getting out, she looked in the mirror and screamed, for, the thing staring back at her, her own reflection, was unrecognizable. It was her, but then again *wasn't*. Her scalp was mottled, and exposed. Her hair, once long and beautiful had fallen out. Her lips had corroded, turning her mouth into a terrifying, toothy grin.

It was still burning, though, and she could feel DreamSparkle's chemicals eating deeper and deeper into her dermis like she was the incredible melting woman.

"Help me!" she yelled, running back to the kitchen, hoping the neighbours might hear.

*I need to do something. It's killing me.* She remembered the magazine ad. *'Call blankety-blank for treatment advice.'*

She fell to her knees and began, frantically, flicking through the magazines, the corners of the pages sticking to her bloody fingertips. Eventually, she found what she was looking for. The ad was still there of course, with the woman wearing the apron, with that same beaming happy smile, with that same voila-there-you-have-it gesture, but it was different somehow. *What was different?* She didn't care. She had the number for the treatment line.

Betty stood up, panicked, the magazine still in hand. She picked up the handset and started dialling. While bashing the numbers with one bloody digit, she realized there was no dial tone. Ned still hadn't called the phone company.

*Fuck!* It dawned on her she wouldn't be calling anyone, and she sank to her knees, letting the handset hang from its cord.

Looking at the magazine again, she noticed why the ad had been so different. *What the fuck?* One side of the DreamSparkle woman's face was red and burned, her mouth, a twisted and bloody maw.

Betty opened another magazine to see if the ad had changed there, too, and it had. She opened another, and another, until she had scrutinized every single one.

They were all different. They'd all changed. But how? Each and every single ad was horrific, showing the apron-adorned DreamSparkle woman, stepping away from their kitchens in various degrees of disintegration, with hideous burns—and it got worse in the later issues. It was like a demented flick book, showing the progressively worsening states of decomposition.

*Who put these magazines here? Is this some kind of sick practical joke?* But then something occurred to her she hadn't noticed before. It wasn't just the same woman in all of the DreamSparkle ads; it was, also, the same kitchen. In fact, it was *her* kitchen. She looked about her—at the counter, the sink, at the kitchen cabinets—and knew it was true.

*Oh Jesus. I'm the woman in the ad.*

"Help!" she screamed, slumping against the kitchen cabinets. "Oh, God, please."

*I'm sorry.* She clutched her burning chest. *I'm sorry I ever slept with Mike Foster. I wished I'd never even heard his name.* The pain was coming in waves, and she knew the final tsunami would be coming soon.

*I love you, Ned. I was a fool not to have realized it. The more I think about it...I've never not loved you.* Her breathing grew laboured. *You and Alex. Oh, my beautiful baby.*

She cried more and more bloody tears. *Wait, what will they think when they come home and find me, or, what's left of me, a melted and bloody mess?*

She laughed a strange sort of laugh, and wondered if, perhaps, she'd already lost the grip on her sanity.

*Nothing a little DreamSparkle can't fix.*

# Gnome

There's a gnome at the end of our back garden; one of those terracotta guys you see with a beard and a funny hat. He was a housewarming gift from my Aunt Tracey, a loving but neurotic woman, with a blue-rinsed hairdo and tuckshop-lady-arms. It was just the sort of impractical gift I'd come to expect from her.

"It's kitsch," she said, that day of the barbecue. "It will bring you good luck."

I looked at the gnome. "It's not exactly *on-brand* for us, Tracey."

She smirked. "Gnomes are lucky. You'll see. Luck of the Irish."

"I thought that was leprechauns?" Michelle said.

Tracey shrugged. "Gnomes too."

I shook my head and returned to flipping burgers on the grill, happy in my ignorance. I wish

I'd known then what I know now. I had no idea of the danger.

Michelle and I met at a wedding. She was in the bridal party, while I was in the band. During one of the breaks, I worked up the nerve to speak to the ebony-haired bridesmaid with sea-blue eyes, and we hit it off. Michelle and I started dating and before long we were living together.

Michelle is a teacher at the local primary school. She's both intelligent, kind, and her smile will light up a room. Always the sensible one, she helped me get my shit together. I never thought I'd settle down but she made it easy.

During our fourth year as a couple, a job opened for Michelle at a school in Toowoomba. We didn't know anybody in T-Bar at the time—except for Aunt Tracey—but the job offered a decent pay rise so we decided to move. The prospect of relocating to a new city was both daunting and exciting.

I'd already switched to packing shelves at Woolies by that point. Michelle encouraged me to quit, though, suggesting I get back into music full-time.

"Try it for a year," Michelle had said. "See if you can make it work."

That was fine by me. I'd planned on setting up a home studio when we arrived in Toowoomba anyway. Over the years I'd penned notebooks full of song lyrics and aspired to make an album. I just had to get my head around the recording software.

Michelle had been hassling me about starting a family. I wasn't keen. Every time she brought it up I'd change the subject. I had reservations about being a dad, wondering if I'd make a good role model. We are all doomed to become our parents, are we not? The relationship I had with my own father was dysfunctional, to say the least—the manic highs and rash decisions: it was exhausting. A situation I was loathe to repeat.

The only thing I got from Dad, other than my good looks and sense of musical timing, was a 1970 Holden HT Monaro GTS 350, which I kept in the driveway.

"Don't be silly," Michelle had said, when she told me she was pregnant. "You'll make a great dad."

I think back to the day of the barbecue all the time. Michelle's dad, Doug, had come down from Caloundra for the weekend. He was a nuggety bloke with a buzz cut, his face weathered and craggy from all the years without sunblock. As a former sparky, he was deliberate, methodical. We couldn't be more different.

Some of the neighbours were there including Mr. Pantelis. He'd brought fresh oranges from his tree. He loved his garden and his vegetables, perhaps, even more than he loved Mrs. Pantelis. She was always yelling something at him in Greek.

I brought the platter of burgers to the trestle table where everyone was sat. The wind picked up and Tracey wrestled with the tablecloth, preventing several paper plates from flying.

Michelle gave me a peck on the cheek before doing a quick lap, making sure everyone's drink was filled. She tapped her fork to the side of a carafe to gain everyone's attention. "I'd like to thank you all for coming today and making us feel welcome. I can't properly express how nice it is to feel we're part of the community. We're looking forward to getting to know all of you individually. Hopefully, there'll be more of these types of events in the future."

"Here, here," someone chimed in.

Michelle cleared her throat. "I've been wrestling with whether or not to say this next thing…"

She glanced at me and I tilted my head offering her encouragement.

"Okay, I'm just going come right out and say it—"

You could hear a pin drop.

"—I'm pregnant."

Everyone cheered, as Michelle and I embraced.

***

Anyway, there the gnome stands, at the end of our backyard, about 18" high, conspicuously positioned in the garden bed between the agapanthus and hydrangeas. He wears a jaunty red cap, a blue smock top, and a pair of shiny gumboots. The fucking thing unsettles me. He vexes me.

That night after the barbecue and after everyone had gone home, I'd finished taking the bin out to the kerb and had returned to the yard, when…

Movement. Out of the corner of my eye. Maybe a shadow. Or, was it just a feeling? My stomach did a backflip and I had actual gooseflesh.

The gnome was there, with his snow-white-whiskers in the Amish style, one hand resting on the handle of a terracotta pitchfork and the other clasping the bowl of a skinny clay pipe. It felt like the bugger was watching me. It was like one of those trick paintings—no matter where I stood his eyes seemed to follow. It was creepy. I swear his clay pipe was sitting at a different angle, too. I went and turned him round so he faced the fence. I felt silly for doing it at the time, but, now, in hindsight…

Inside, Michelle sat cross-legged watching Netflix. I kissed her and joined her on the couch, forgetting about the gnome, worrying, instead, whether I would make a good dad.

***

In the morning, I got up to feed Michelle's dog, a Pomeranian named Bella. I'd never purposefully own a dog. They're unhygienic and slobber over everything. I guess I'm more of a cat person. In any case, during the divvying up of household chores, it fell to me to feed Bella.

While pouring kibble into a bowl, I glanced at the gnome. His eyes seemed to twinkle and gleam, his rosy-red, cheeks were turned up in a smile. Or, was it a jeer?

*Unbelievable. The bugger's changed positions.*

He had somehow turned back round and was staring at me with his beady little eyes.

Bella stood with her hackles up, growling, equally unsettled by it.

"Hey, babe?" I called.

Michelle was humming to herself, inside the recesses of the house.

"Yeah?"

"Did you move the gnome this morning?"

"What?"

I went inside. The screen door swung shut behind me. "The garden gnome, did you move it?"

"Now, why would I move that silly thing?"

I rubbed the top of my head. "I swear—"

The gnome, was in its usual spot, looking ordinary. Michelle gave me a sideways look. I could tell what she was thinking.

*I'm not my dad,* I thought.

***

Days later, I stepped out to water the plants in the backyard—the garden hose had a trigger, like a pistol. The Australian summer can play havoc on your garden if you're not careful. I mean we are in the middle of a drought. We weren't as affected as the inland areas but were still restricted to watering before ten in the morning. Bella was outside with me, chewing a rope toy.

I started watering over by the lavender bushes, working my way, slowly, back.

Gardening is a favorite pastime for some people. I guess it's part of that Aussie dream isn't it— having your own place, surrounded by a garden? But it wasn't for me. I could take it or leave it. I'd rather play guitar or tinker on the Monaro. I kept up with it out of habit I guess. It was simply a question of maintenance.

When I got to the agapanthus and the hydrangeas, I was surprised to see they were shriveled and dying. It was as if they'd not been watered in yonks, which was odd because I'd only just watered them the previous morning.  They had been tall and strong, despite the heat. Something was wrong. I scanned the garden bed around the gnome. The patch of grass around our mate, the gnome, had yellowed, as if someone had hit it with Roundup. This didn't compute. Then it twigged…

*Bloody Bella.*

I went inside. Michelle was in the kitchen, washing dishes by hand because the machine was on the fritz.

"Your dog's been peeing on the garden," I said.

Michelle huffed a laugh. "Excuse me? My dog? Bella's *our* dog, thanks very much. Besides, isn't she supposed to go in the garden?"

"Yeah, but…on the lawn, not on the garden bed. She's killing the agapanthus."

She put her hands on her hips. "What do you propose we do about it?"

"I don't know," I said. "Maybe I should put up a temporary fence?"

She shrugged. "If you think that'll work?"

***

I made a trip to Bunnings the following weekend, returning with a bunch of garden stakes and chicken wire. I finished putting up the makeshift fence, to keep Bella away from the garden, then, settled into doing maintenance on the Monaro. I had my head under the bonnet, tinkering with the carburetor air cleaner when I heard a familiar voice.

"Will?"

It gave me such a start I bumped my head.

It was Mr. Pantelis, looking flustered.

"Oh, hey, George," I said, rubbing my head.

"Will…" he looked down. "I wonder what I've done to annoy you?"

"Huh? What do you mean?"

"Well, just look at the state of these tomatoes." He took a couple from a hessian bag, waving them under my nose. They had an unpleasant odor and were discoloured, wrinkled, and mushy. They had visible patches of mould as if they'd been stored in the bag for weeks without refrigeration.

"I don't get it," I said, pinching my nose due to the smell.

"I picked these off the vine this morning. And what about these cucumbers?" he said, producing two more equally degraded-looking vegetables.

I grimaced. "George, I—um…I—don't know what you're getting at. I don't see how your vegetables have anything to do with me."

"They were fine before you moved in. You—you've been using poison. I found these all along our back fence. Whatever you're spraying you need to stop it, it's leeching through to our place. You're killing all our vegetables."

I took a step back, shaking my head. "George, I swear to you, we haven't been spraying anything. I couldn't even if I wanted to. Michelle won't allow it—herbicides are bad for the baby. Also, why would I…To spite you?"

He blinked. "Well, how did my vegetables get like this."

I shrugged. "Some sort of fungus maybe? Perhaps the—"

*The gnome.*

My mouth was suddenly very dry.

***

I went to work on the Monaro the next morning but was surprised to find a dirty great big scratch down one side, as if someone'd keyed it. I mean, I could have cried. *Bastards. Probably kids in the neighborhood up to mischief.* If only we'd installed a security camera. I would have loved to catch the little shits in the act. But it wasn't to be I guess.

We didn't have the money for a professional body shop, so I had to do the repair myself. I spent the rest of that morning trying to match the right color of touch-up paint at Supercheap Auto. It was a real pain in the neck.

But when I came home I found Michelle on the bed. She was deathly pale and complaining of cramps. We were worried we might lose the baby, so I rushed her to the obstetrician to get her checked. They said it was common to experience cramping as well as some spotting in the early stages of pregnancy, a false alarm. We both breathed a sigh of relief.

***

Weeks later, I finished converting the third bedroom into a home recording studio. I'd hung all my guitars on the wall using hooks: the obligatory acoustic, the 12-string I picked up in Sydney, and the Fender Jaguar, with the sunburst finish. They looked great on display, next to the posters of ACDC and Cold Chisel.

Michelle had already bought a bassinet online and had set it in the corner. I knew it was only a matter of time before my would-be studio would be repurposed as a nursery. This increased the urgency. I had to finish an album before the baby arrived.

Late one night, while doing some recording— I was finally getting the hang of the software, by mixing, and adjusting the input levels—I happened to glance out the window and saw, staring back at me from the end of the garden, a pair of red, glowing, eyes.

I froze—feeling like every ounce of blood had just drained from my extremities. Peering into the inky darkness, I recognized a familiar visage. It was the bearded, rosy-cheeked face of the gnome.

*I must be losing it.*

A wisp of smoke issued from its clay pipe.

I closed the blinds with a jerk—as if this would undo what I'd just seen.

***

That night I had a fitful sleep, tossing and turning, waking in fits and starts. The air was close and my skin was clammy. I slept on top of the covers, staring at the ceiling, listening to the gentle purrs of Michelle snoring beside me.

When I did finally drift off, I dreamt of an immense garden. Only I was in miniature. I'd shrunk down to the size of an ant so that every blade of grass towered like the tallest redwood. I called for Michelle but she was nowhere to be seen.

Soon I became aware of a giant shadow, looming. I was being stalked by some-*thing*. I ran and ran, all the while yelling, "Oh, God. Help! Please help!"

All in vain.

I tripped and fell. While peering between the blades of grass, I saw a giant red cap approaching. The things footsteps were like thunder and shook the ground so violently I thought the whole world might fall apart. It was such a vivid dream I wondered if my dream-self would ever rejoin my physical body still slumbering on the mattress in our bedroom.

I became aware of a presence in the room where Michelle and I slept. It's weight settled on my chest, perching like some predatory bird, its cold, terracotta hands encircling my neck, choking. In my dream, I was screaming.

I awoke gasping for air.

"What's the matter?" Michelle said, alarmed.

A tiny shadow flitted past the doorway, or so I thought, and I heard the titter of high-pitched laughter.

***

As the days and weeks passed, I was plagued by similar dreams, which increased my stress and anxiety. Unsettled, traumatized, I began to obsess about the gnome.

I scoured the Internet for information, and found the following:

*Gnome (noun). Nisse in Norway, or Tomte in Sweden are a species of diminutive beings common to Nordic and Scandinavian folklore. They inhabit the interior of the earth but frequently occupy the houses or barns of humans. Across Scandinavia, people believe gnomes are mischievous spirits, with often dark or evil intentions.*

"What are you doing?" Michelle asked, coming into the studio, her hand supporting her now very pregnant belly.

"Just trying to get inspired, y'know?" I said, hurriedly closing the search window.

"That didn't look music-related." She looked at my guitars still on their hangers.

"I'm waiting for my muse."

She frowned. "Well, don't wait too long—Look, I know you've stopped recording. And you're not sleeping. What's bothering you?"

I thought about telling her but couldn't. "I appreciate you asking but I just need space right now."

"I bet you didn't even hand out those flyers for the guitar lessons like I asked you—Fair enough if you don't feel like recording anymore, but you're not working, and you're not pulling your weight. If you don't straighten up and fly right soon then we might need to reassess where things are headed. We have a baby on the way, a baby that needs its daddy."

I put the gnome out with the garbage that very night. I thought that would be the end of it. It wasn't.

***

The next morning, I went to the local shops and pinned a flyer advertising private guitar lessons on the local community board. It wasn't much but it was a start. I promised myself I'd make things up to Michelle.

While arriving home, however, I noticed a very odd thing; the garbage collectors had been and gone, had emptied the bins, and set the gnome back down on the kerb. So, when I pulled the Monaro into the driveway the gnome was stood there looking at me, with that same sly, wicked grin.

The only thing I could figure was maybe the garbage collection guys, having seen the gnome intact, must have wondered why anybody would be throwing out such an interesting and pristine item, and set it back on the kerb.

Puzzled by this, and not able to think of a better solution, I put it back in its usual spot and threw a tarp over it.

*You'll have to stay there till next garbage day.*

I found Bella, the Pomeranian, in the yard a short time later, broken and bloodied—the poor thing had been pulverized by someone or some-*thing*. Its insides were dashed out. I had a heck of a time trying to settle Michelle when she came home.

"Why would anybody do this?" she kept repeating, amidst tears.

I knew it wasn't any one person or persons responsible. It had to be the gnome. It was getting back at me for putting it on the kerb. It wanted revenge.

***

By this time all the plants in the garden had shriveled and died, and the grass had yellowed—reminding me of a contagion. I couldn't pinpoint exactly when it happened. It was a slow spread.

It was around that time, too, that Michelle had her miscarriage.

It was a dark time. She cried and cried for days. I did my best to console her, to comfort her, but it was no use. What was there to do, exactly? We were both grieving. She'd had this thing growing inside her, and then it was gone. That sort of trauma affects a person.

The sense of loss we felt was acute. I can only imagine what it must have been like for her, losing the baby. The physical connection a mother has—it's different—it must have been unbearable.

We fought more. I still wasn't working and was drinking. She'd claimed I'd become obsessed by the gnome, that I'd become *erratic*.

Well, I knew more than the next person about erratic behaviour. When I was a kid, Dad frequently had *episodes*, hallucinations. It was a fault in his brain chemistry. I remember…

*The school bus dropped me off down the street. I should've known something was off, as the front door had been left ajar. I flung my school bag down. The furniture in the living room had been upended.*

*"Dad, you okay?"*

*He stood in front of the hallway mirror, muttering to himself.*

*"Will? You're home early," he said, distracted. "Damn Feds," looking back at the mirror. "They've bugged the house."*

*"Dad, where's, Mum? I think you might need—"*

*"Fucking Feds!" He struck out with his fist and the mirror shattered, sending fragments across the floor.*

Dad never could tune out his inner voices. It made me wonder. Psychosis can run in families. *Am I going mad?*

***

More days came and went and I became convinced the gnome was the source of our problems. It was a curse of some kind. I couldn't just throw it away. The damn thing had a knack of returning.

I trawled the Internet looking for answers, finding articles about theosophy, Tibetan mantras, witchcraft, and vampirism—amongst other subjects. But it wasn't until I read an article about possessed objects that things started to fit into place. I read how, during one of the four degrees of demonic possession—*infestation*—the afflicted might hear footsteps, voices, or smell odors; how they might even see objects move—real haunted house shit.

I thought back to dad. He claimed he saw objects move.

*Am I crazy for buying into this?*

I shrugged it off.

*Infestation*, apparently affected *objects* rather than people, and could lead to the object becoming possessed by a spirit or demon. I thought of the gnome. This last explanation, although seemingly impossible, was, perhaps, the most probable.

*I have to destroy it*, I thought. But wasn't clear how.

Then I read an article by Anton Von Meter—an occultist and self-proclaimed wizard. Von Meter claimed to have destroyed a living statue by separating the pieces, burning it, and then sprinkling it with holy water.

*It's worth a try.*

But where would I find holy water? I couldn't just rock up to a Catholic Church and ask a Priest. How would that even go? The idea was laughable. No, I had to think of another way.

I found a recipe for holy water online. It sounded easy enough: a little water, some salt, a blessing.

That clinched it. I was going to destroy the gnome.

***

One weekend, Michelle's Dad came to visit. From my position on a deck chair in the yard, I heard Aunt Tracey and Michelle conversing with him in the kitchen. I pretended not to hear and went about my business of staring at the gnome.

*You won't be grinning for much longer, you little, fucker.* I chuckled and took a swig of beer.

The screen door swung open and shut. It was Doug.

"Can I talk to you a moment, son?" he said, gruffly, shuffling up beside me.

"Suit yourself," I said, motioning to the other deck chair.

His knees cracked as he settled into it.

"We're all worried about you, Will," he said. "Michelle especially."

I ignored him, still fixated on the gnome.

"It's unhealthy you sitting out here all the time, by yourself." He rubbed the back of his neck. "Michelle's upset. She said you've been seeing things, hearing things. Is that right?"

I scoffed. Still staring at the gnome, I was certain it would move. It had to. And if it did, Doug was there, he'd see it and I'd have proof. But alas the evil shit was too clever. It remained motionless, standing there in the garden bed, staring right back at me.

"Are you listening to me, Will?" Doug said. "I think you need help. You might need—"

"A shrink?" I said indignantly. "No way."

He stood. "Listen, I guess it's no secret that I've never liked you. I always held my tongue. You're not good enough for Michelle and never will be in my opinion. But, the girl loves you." He shrugged. "Don't ask me why. The heart wants what it wants, I guess. We all lie in the beds we make for ourselves. But if you disappoint my daughter…so help me…"

"Fuck off, old man," I fired back, with enough venom to take down a water buffalo. I'd had a gut full.

Doug's face went crimson with anger, but he calmed himself and went back inside.

Moments later, Michelle came out and sat on the other deck chair.

"I'm leaving, Will," she said. "I'm going to stay with Dad."

I was devastated, but hid it well.

"Are you going to stop this behavior?" she asked.

I said nothing.

She drew in her breath sharply. "I thought you loved me."

I could hear her weeping as she and Doug left, and it took all my resolve not to go running after her.

*It's for the best,* I tried to convince myself. *She needs to get far away from here. Somewhere safe. Somewhere the gnome can't find her.*

***

So, here I am standing in the yard next to a rusty, old wheelbarrow. Michelle's gone.  The house is empty. Most of the stuff was hers anyway.

*I'm slipping. Jesus, what if they're right?* I shift the weight of the hammer in my hand, still trying to catch my breath. *What if this is all in my head?*

What's left of the gnome is in charred and broken pieces at the bottom of the wheelbarrow. Despite the hammer blows, the petrol, and setting it alight, I still recognise one of the shards as the gnome's mouth. It glistens in the moonlight.

*Cheeky, fucker's still grinning.*

The fire's gone out and it's started to rain.

I say the words and pour the holy water. *It's done.*

The Monaro's parked in the driveway. I get in, throwing my duffle bag stuffed full of clothes in the back. *Caloundra's not far. I'll be there in a couple of hours. Maybe Michelle will take me back.*

I turn the key in the ignition and the engine roars to life. I put it in gear and roll out of the driveway. *I'm coming, Michelle.*

I make it to Gatton Esk Road.

*The nightmare's over. Nothing behind me but empty road.* I adjust the rearview mirror. *Odd.* I catch the whiff of something.

The faint odor of petrol and smoke. The back seat folds down.

*Oh, Jesus. I can hear it crawling from the boot.* In the mirror, I see its little head and its beady, red eyes—

# Idol Hands

*Proverbs 16:27 Idle hands are the devil's workshop; idle lips are his mouthpiece*

Slowly working my way back to consciousness, buoyed on an ocean of endless night, I become aware of my own body again. My skin is alive with the pricking and tingling of a thousand pins and needles. Nausea. Confusion. I feel the polished, concrete floor beneath me. My head is pounding. I taste vomit but manage to hold it down.

*Where am I?* I think to myself, smacking my lips, the corners of my mouth all gummy. Blinking a few times I clear my blurry vision. I'm already sitting upright.

I reel back and let out a shriek. Several paces away there's a face, passive and emotionless. I realize it isn't real. *It's just a mannequin.* I laugh at myself but the laughter dies on my lips. There are in fact rows of mannequins: some of them hanging from racks; others on stands and in various stages of completion, without heads or hands—all of them naked. The mannequin in front of me is missing its arms like a grotesque Venus de Milo.

I must be in a basement or warehouse of some kind, a room about the size of your average *Denny's* restaurant. The otherwise darkened space is illuminated, all around, by rows of burning candles, like a Sunday mass, and the air is fragrant with the aroma of burning incense. By the dim candlelight, I make out detail from the clutter: bags of plaster; boxes filled with packing Styrofoam; a bin filled with discarded fiberglass legs, arms, and hands. In the shadows, there is a wall taken-up by a blinking, humming machine. Over by a workbench is a half-done clay sculpture. Fashion clippings and magazine cutouts are pinned to a corkboard above the workspace. And there are the mannequins, rows of inanimate bodies, expressionless faces, watching, mocking.

I try to move but can't. My hands are bound. *I'm tied to a radiator in someone's basement.* "Shit!" The realization hits me like a falling anvil. I try to squirm free. *Stop it, Alice. This isn't getting you anywhere.*

I take a deep breath. "Hello."

No response.

"Think it through, Alice," I say to myself. "How did you get here? What was the last thing you remember?" *I met with Abbi and Reese. Abbi had just gotten a raise. That's right. We were having drinks, celebrating. What was the name of that place?* I winced. *Hell, how many drinks did I have?*

"Hello?" I say again.

Nothing.

I adjust the way I'm sitting and with shaky hands, I try and wriggle free from my restraints. The cable ties—if that's what they are—are tightly secured. *I've got to get out of here.*

Then I remember. While Abbi and Reese were on the dance floor, bumping and grinding and getting down with a couple of Wall Street flunkies, I was on the veranda with a guy.

*What was his name again? Barry? Billy? He seemed harmless. He didn't seem interested in chatting me up. What was it he did again? Fashion? Art? Fuck, I should pay more attention.*

I moan. *He bought me a drink. Could he have slipped me something? Freaking Rohypnol, maybe? Jesus. There was a lot of noise and movement in the club. I could have looked away. He had opportunity.*

I struggle, but the cable ties cut deeper into my wrists. I look in desperation at a set of sharpened, sculpting tools lying on top of a nearby table. *If only I could reach one, maybe I could cut myself loose.* I kick out with my legs knocking over a candle. The flame flickers before snuffing out in a pool of wax.

"Oh good, you're awake," a male voice says.

There's a figure in the doorway. I can't make out his face, as it's mostly in shadow.

"Who are you? What do you want?"

He shifts his weight. "All in good time, Alice. You can call me Billy."

"Billy?" I repeat. "The guy from the club?"

"Yeah, Alice, the guy from the club."

"Oh, Jesus. Please don't hurt me."

"Relax," he says, raising his hand in a quieting gesture. "If I wanted you dead, you'd be dead already."

I start crying and let out a sound like a whimper.

"Easy," he says, stepping from the shadows. "I need you for something important, you're going to be a sort of…witness."

He is of medium height and build, dressed in a denim shirt and jeans, with closely shorn hair, unremarkable looking.

"A witness?"

He nods. Coming closer, his dark and gleaming eyes devoid of all empathy.

"Yes, you're lucky. You could say that you've been chosen—chosen to witness something extraordinary." He leans in to brush a stray strand of hair from my face.

I shrink away from his touch. The scent of musky cologne lingers.

"Don't worry—I've got no interest in you sexually if that's what you're worried about." He laughs.

My chest tightens and I'm shaking.

He steps away. Beside him is the mannequin I thought of, earlier, as the Venus de Milo. At once humanlike and alien, its features are detailed but with the unnatural pallor of a corpse. It stands, watching, a mockery of life.

I can't help but shudder.

"I see you two have already met?" He looks first at Venus then at me. "I'm kidding." He grins. "I know it's just a mannequin. How you supposed to talk with a mannequin? You two are gonna become better acquainted, though. That's for sure."

I try to look away. "Please. You can just let me go. I won't call the cops. It'll be like this never happened."

He puts a finger to his lips and shushes me. "You're embarrassing yourself."

I change the position of my legs to help with the growing numbness.

"She doesn't look like much, now, does she?" he says, gesturing to Venus. He goes to a nearby bin and retrieves a couple of fiberglass arms. With an expert twist and shove he affixes them to the mannequin. "There you go. That looks much better, don't you think?"

I start crying again. Tears cascade down my cheeks.

"What do you think of my workshop? Nice?" He takes a stick of chalk from his pocket and begins drawing a wide, circle on the floor, with the mannequin at its center.

"Yeah, it's all mine," he says, continuing with the circle. "From here, I supply mannequins to all the major department stores in the city. Strange, huh—considering Mom said I'd never amount to anything?"

Having finished with the circle, he starts adding some intricate symbols and characters.

"Mom was the clingy type," he continues. "Demanding, y'know? She wouldn't allow me to go out or have any friends. But, she was a smart woman. Do you know what Mother used to say to me?"

I shake my head.

"She'd say, 'Billy, you've got to take life into your own hands. Be the artist of your own destiny.'" He finishes drawing the symbols, discarding the chalk, brushing the excess dust from his hands. "And so here I am, a sculptor."

He looks at me. "Mother was always literal." He chuckles.

"Yep. You have to be a special kind of artist," he says. "First, it starts with the clay sculpture, then a fiberglass mold, followed by the sanding and spraying. From one mold I can make hundreds of mannequins. It's not easy. You need an artistic flair. You need to have an eye for movement and flow. You need to envision the right look, the right aesthetic."

"Please, Billy, you've got to let me go," I say.

Ignoring me he says, "That's me I *create*. I'm a creator. Just as the Jewish and Christian God molded Adam and Eve from a lump of clay, I breathe life *here* into these mannequins." He spreads his arms wide signifying the magnitude of his work, and for a moment he is lost in rapture. "Don't believe me? Well, you'll see. Just as the Jewish Rabbi made a fearsome golem, I, too, will imbue life into this mannequin."

"Pleease!" I say.

"Shut up," he says, taking a sword from the workbench. He swings it over his head with a flourish. "I don't have to do anything!"

A warm sensation spreads in my lap.

"Oops. Scared you did I?" he says, holding the sword, now, loose by his side. "Never mind. It happens to the best of us."

I grit my teeth. *Fuck, you, you fucking psycho.*

"Since I was a boy," he says, tracing the edges of the circle with the sword's point, "I've had a fascination with the occult. I read every book I could find on the subject. I'd spend all day at the public library. Then one day, I came across a particularly ancient and rotting tome, a volume which made mention of the goddess, Vharakhee, and the ancient rites to summon her."

I shake my head, astonished at the lunacy of my captor.

Perhaps, sensing my skepticism, Billy says, "That's alright." He finishes with the sword and places it on the workbench. "You don't understand the significance of this moment. It's the seventh night of the eleventh month, when the stars, Riox and Yaud, align, and the moon is full. It is written that Vharakhee, The Accursed One, will be reborn. That's what this is you see," he says referring to the mannequin. "It's an effigy."

He takes a power drill from the workbench and drills a hole for Venus's mouth. "Just a little prayer," he says, inserting a scrap of paper. "I suppose you'd call it a spell."

"I'm going to conjure Vharakhee by completing the ritual," he says. "She will manifest *here* in the mannequin. It will be a living statue. And I will be the right hand of a god."

"You're crazy," I say.

"Crazy?" He scoffs. "Crazy smart, maybe."

"Even if this hocus pocus stuff is real, Billy, why would you—"

"Because I can," he counters.

I feel like I'm about to vomit and my life begins to flash before my eyes. I think back to the events that have led me here. I think of Mom; Dad; and Ruby, our Labrador. I think of elementary school and the years growing up in Chesterfield, New Jersey. I think of my sister, Megan, pushing me down the stairs when I was eight. I think of my first boyfriend, my first job, and my first apartment.

Mom was an ultra-religious-type. She'd call me a whore for wearing lipstick and would tell me I was going to Hell for the TV shows I watched, and for the books I read.

Dad, on the other hand, was my rock, my island. A local TV weatherman for PBS, he was filled with mirth and wisdom, and little sayings that made me who I am today.

Billy takes out a book and begins to read from it in a weird language. He's chanting, now, and the air seems to swirl, charged with electricity.

I see the sculpting tools on the table again. *If only I could reach them.*

I think back to high school when Megan read my personal diary aloud to the entire senior year class. I remember that day and afterward coming home. I was inconsolable. Only Dad could talk me down…

"It was horrible, Dad."

We sat on the edge of my bed in our tiny three-bedder in Chesterfield, and I spilled everything that was on my mind.

"I can't go back there. I'll run away before I go back there again."

He sighed, wrapping an arm around my shoulder. "I know, peach, but you can't let it get to you. Bad things are going to happen in life no matter what, whether you're prepared for it or not. But whatever you do, you have to decide to make things better. Destiny is not a matter of chance. It's a matter of choice."

My mind snaps back to the present.

"Why won't you just let me go?" I say.

Billy makes a face as if considering whether or not to answer. "To summon Vharakhee I need an offering. Now, most gods need an offering of some kind or other. Some like the first fruits of the harvest. Some like grain, wine, or honey. While some require an offering of a different kind. A greater sacrifice. You see, Vharakhee requires an offering of human blood. A lot of blood. Your blood."

I cry and wail, and thrash around trying to get free of my bonds. "Let me go you, psycho motherfucker!" But it's useless. I only succeed in tiring myself and the cable ties cut even deeper into my wrists.

"Are you finished," he says, amused.

"You said you weren't going to hurt me. You said you needed a witness?"

"I lied," he says, shrugging, and places a black-stoned amulet about his neck.

"Fuck you!" I hock a gob of spit in his direction.

"Careful." He grins. "We're going to need you hydrated if we're to bleed you soon." And he continues to read from his book.

I slump against the radiator. I feel tired, so very tired. *Most people die at home or in a hospital. But I'm going to die tied to this radiator—the fucking indignity of it.*

I hear a voice in my mind, say, *'What are you doing? Are you just going to sit there?'* I know it isn't Dad, but it sure sounds like him. 'Think it through,' he says, in his usual self-assured tone.

*It's useless,* I think.

*'What do you mean it's useless? What kind of talk is that?'*

*I'm tied up, Dad, and Billy the psycho sorcerer is going to kill me.*

*'You have a choice: sit there and die, or, you can act.'*

And I realize that, although I am trapped, I can do something about it. My entire life I've been trapped in some way or another: trapped by my bullying sister, trapped in Jersey, trapped by my job, trapped in relationships. But, now, I'm strong. I've got to escape. I must survive.

*'Look,'* says Dad's voice.

I see the candles and suddenly it's clear what I must do.

I change the way I'm sitting, and while Billy is occupied, reading and chanting from his book, I surreptitiously knock over a candle. Its flame falters.

*Please don't go out.*

The candle rolls and I guide it with the edge of my shoe so it passes underneath me. I grab it with my fingertips. The flame has gone out but the wax is still hot. I hold it to the cable ties around my wrists. My skin blisters, but it's also burning through the ties.

"What are you doing?" says Billy, storming over.

*God, no!*

I attempt to scratch his face, but he's on me in an instant, grabbing a fistful of my hair and holding a curved dagger to my throat. "Where d'ya think you're going?"

I glare at him.

"Cheeky," he says, finding the broken ties, musing at the broken ends.

He ties the next ones extra tight.

A short time later, while touching his amulet and reading from his book, Billy lets out an ululating cry. Blinding arcs of energy shoot forth across the room releasing a hail of sparks. A moat of flame spirals above us, intense and shimmering, and there is a moaning, wheezing tortured breath like that of an abyssal creature.

My heart is pounding.

The nearby table is knocked over by the turbulent air and vibration, scattering the sculpture tools across the floor. A clay-cutting knife rolls in my direction. I check to see if Billy notices. He doesn't. I grab it and begin to cut the cable ties.

I look up. The eyes of the mannequin—those, now, horribly bloodshot eyes—start to move. It looks at me and I scream.

A moment later my hands are free. I spring to my feet but Billy is between the doorway and me, blocking my escape. He grabs the sword. I'm holding the sculpting tool in front of me determined to stab if he comes closer.

"You bitch!" he says.

The mannequin has started to move. I see its humanlike eyes, so full of hatred, the eyes of a god. They roll in their sockets and stare in my direction.

Billy rushes me. I drop and stab him. His momentum keeps going, though, and we wrestle to the floor, knocking over the mannequin. It smashes into four pieces on the concrete floor.

"What have you done?" Billy screams.

With renewed energy and the strength of a madman, he rolls on top of me kicking and punching.

I try to grab at anything—his hair, his clothes, whatever—just to get him off me. I grab hold of the amulet and wrench it from his neck.

He hits me again and again. I taste my own blood in my mouth as he beats me. Blood spills on the amulet. *I've changed from that small girl, weak-willed, a shrinking violet. I broke free. I might die but I'm going to die free. I chose. I made my choice.*

I feel a strange state coming over me. A fierce power surges through me. My veins feel like they're on fire. I'm burning. I'm burning. I feel disconnected from my soul. Am I going crazy? It's like I'm someone else completely. I'm overcome with rage and hatred. I stand bolt upright, lifting Billy aloft like a ragdoll, a plaything.

The look of surprise on his face is delicious. I am lost. I am not me. I am a passenger, but I am gleeful.

Using my mind, I throw him to the wall pinning him with his own sword. He gasps, struggles for a moment, then, goes limp.

The army of silent mannequins look on with mute appreciation.

I have killed him. I killed Billy the psycho sorcerer and I loved it. A part of me is exhilarated, ecstatic. But another part of me—Alice, the passenger—is sad. For, I will never be the small girl again. For all my flaws. For all my weaknesses. I'm no longer who I was. I am the vessel for an avenging spirit. I raise my hands before my face.

I am the goddess Vharakhee.

# Darker Skies

Astronomer Emma Price Ph.D. sat at her desk in the office space of Warrundella Observatory, deep in thought, lamplight illuminating her face, a complex array of radio waves displayed in a visual on her computer monitor. She rolled her swivel chair to face another monitor displaying a star chart. *What am I doing here?* she thought, her fingertips tapping out a clickety klack tune on the keyboard. *All this extra dish time. Mum was right. I should've been a medical doctor, or an architect.* Behind her, the blinds of the largest window were open, revealing a colossal radio telescope dish silhouetted against the night sky.

Emma reached down and gave her dog a scratch behind the ears, an old lab named Lyra who was fast asleep at her heels. She sat back up and adjusted her glasses. The observatory was run by the CSIRO (Commonwealth Scientific and Industrial

Research Organization) as part of a network of radio telescopes, used in astronomical research. The telescope had been contracted to project Breakthrough Listen.

She moved the mouse cursor a few degrees of ascension while sipping coffee from a novelty mug.

"TCHK TCHK KHLAK."

A loud sound emitted from the speakers on the wall.

She dropped the mug and it shattered on the floor. "No way! No fucking way." Dashing back to the first monitor, she saw there was a solid spike on the display. She entered a few hasty keystrokes, and, outside, the monstrous dish of the radio telescope began to shift with a mechanical whir. The dish moved one way and the signal dropped away. Another few keystrokes, though, and the signal was good.

She clicked a button and started recording.

"TCHK TCHK KHLAK, TCHK TCHK KHLAK, TCHK TCHK KHLAK..."

Moments later the sound stopped.

Emma's heart was beating fast. Brushing the hair from her face, she picked up the phone and dialed her boss in Ulambi. It went straight to voicemail.

"Warwick? Hi, it's me. If you're there pick up?"

Nothing.

"Sorry for calling so late, but it's important." She took a deep breath. "You're not going to believe the signal I just picked up. It's a non-random, non-earth-based signal. Are you there? Hey–pick up."

Again nothing.

*It doesn't matter,* she thought, hanging up the phone. *If you won't come to the mountain—I'm bringing the mountain to you.* Clicking download she saved the recording to a portable hard drive. Emma grabbed her handbag and keys and made a beeline for the front door.

The outside car park was empty except for her Subaru. She clicked the fob on her key ring and its lights flashed on and off. It was a warm night. A halo of moths circled the overhead fluorescent street lamp. She heard the rumble of thunder and knew a storm was on its way. Emma let Lyra jump into the passenger seat before climbing behind the wheel. She turned on the engine, then paused for a moment. By hitting the roads of the national park at night, she risked a kangaroo being drawn to the headlights. But it was a risk worth taking, considering the magnitude of what she had just discovered. She stamped on the accelerator, the tyres of the SUV kicking up dust and gravel as she went. A spattering of raindrops appeared on the windscreen, which quickly turned into a torrent. She tightened her grip on the steering wheel. The road was unpaved. *I'm going too fast,* she thought, as she mounted a crest. She turned on the high beams. *Bloody hell.* She glanced at her handbag on the passenger seat and thought of its important contents. *I hope he's still awake,* she thought, adjusting the rear view mirror. She could barely contain her own excitement. Her hands were shaking. *Warwick's a habitual night owl. He has to be awake. He's probably watching the football.*

The road narrowed into a bumpy dirt track, virtually impassible except for 4WD vehicles, with dense underbrush on either side. Some of the roads to Ulambi had remained closed due to the bushfires several years earlier. Falling trees were a concern in these fire-affected areas. The dirt had already turned to mud. She watched carefully to ensure she didn't skid out.

She caught a glimpse of movement from the corner of her eye as something dashed in front of her. It happened in a blur. Her SUV smashed into whatever it was at full speed. There was a sickening thud. She screamed. The thing rolled up the bonnet and smashed through the windscreen. A splinter of glass cut her brow. She slammed on the brakes and the vehicle came to a skidding halt.

The thing was still wedged on the bonnet. She recognized what looked like a paw protruding through the windscreen, now a cobweb of broken glass. She felt dazed, breathless. After applying the hand break, she got out.

In ambient light from her headlights she could make out the lifeless stare of a big eastern grey kangaroo. The dumb things were known for darting out diagonally in front of cars. Blood dripped from its mouth intermingling with the rain. The thing was dead as disco. She felt her brow and there was blood on her fingertips. *Could've been worse,* she thought. *The car is totaled.* The front was all stove in. *No way is it going to start again.* She sighed. *I might have to spend the night out here.*

Suddenly there was a rustling from the bushes and a single emu stepped onto the track moving briskly, followed by another; then there was a kangaroo; and then a crawling koala; all within the space of a few moments. *What the fuck?* she thought. *What's going on with the wildlife around here?* She suddenly felt very uneasy, so she got back in the car and tried the radio.

***

"Warrundella National Park is the premier dark sky park in the southern hemisphere," Jonesy said, projecting his voice. "Do you know what that means?" It was early morning, he'd been talking for fifteen minutes, and the class of school kids were already showing glazed-over expressions of boredom.

Miss Green, their pretty yet bookish, fifth-grade teacher gave him a smile of encouragement. Jonesy shuffled his feet. The ground was still wet from the storm during the previous night—the folks at the weather bureau had called it a mini-tornado.

"Warrundella attracts astronomers and astronomy enthusiasts from all around the world. Thanks to the low light pollution, and its height above sea level, more stars are visible here than at any other latitude."

The kid closest to him smacked on some gum.

It happened like this every month or so: a busload of city school children would arrive; he would trot out the same over-rehearsed spiel, taking them on a tour of the park, and tell them all about the local flora and fauna. The National Parks Service introduced the initiative the previous year. Despite the children's disinterest, it had quickly become his favorite duty as a park ranger. He hoped to encourage, in them, a love of the great outdoors.

"Wildlife you might expect to see during your visit include the Wedge-tailed Eagle, Kookaburras, the Tawny Frogmouth—"

"Koalas?" asked a pale girl with pimples. Her hair was in braids with butterfly hair clips. It was clear she'd taken tremendous care in picking out what she was wearing.

*Highschool is such a popularity contest.*

"Will we see koalas?" she repeated.

"Possibly," Jonesy said.

There was a burst of radio static. "Are you there?"

Jonesy unhooked the radio from his belt and thumbed the button. "Go ahead, mate." It was unusual for Dazza, one of the other park rangers, to be calling at that time.

*Kish*—"What's your 20?"

Jonesy mouthed the word *sorry* to Miss Green. She waved it off, shepherding the kids to one side.

"I'm with that school group at Banksia Ridge."

"Change of plan, mate. Someone's broken down at Cedar Creek. We're gonna need you to shoot over and assist."

"No worries. I'll head off now. See you back at the Visitors Center. Over." He returned the radio to his belt.

"Sounds important," Miss Green said.

He nodded. "Think you can make your way back to the coach okay?"

***

*Where the bloody hell has this joker broken down?*

Jonesy stretched the map on the dashboard while keeping a steady hand on the wheel. Little more than a bumpy dirt track, the road to Cedar Creek could be treacherous at the best of times. But then, after the storm, the road was scattered with loose leaves and debris.

Lines of gum trees fringed the roadside swaying in the frigid morning breeze, casting corrugated shadows. Several times along the way, Jonesy had to stop the jeep to let a kangaroo or an emu pass—which he thought was unusual, considering normally they were such shy and retiring animals and went out of their way to avoid people.

Over the next crest was a jackknifed SUV with a smashed windscreen and something on the bonnet.

"You're kidding," he said, recognizing the car.

The driver's side opened and Emma Price got out. Her hair was disheveled. She wore her trademark plaid shirt over a white cotton tee, shorts, and hiking boots.

Emma was an astronomer who worked at the observatory. They had been an item, until she blew him off, deciding to concentrate on her work.

"Fuck me dead," he muttered, pulling up behind the SUV. He forced a smile. He needn't have bothered, though. Emma rolled her eyes.

He picked up the radio. "Dazza? You there?"

Pause.

"Yeah, mate. What's up?"

"You, fuck knuckle. You could have told me who I was picking up."

Laughter came back on the radio.

"Don't laugh you, dopey bugger. You could have told me."

"Sorry, mate. I missed that. Say again. You're breaking up."

"You're a deadset cunt, y'know that?"

More laughter.

Jonesy returned the radio to its cradle and got out of the car. "Hey, Em."

"It had to be you of course."

"Are you okay?" he said, noticing blood, brushing her hair aside.

"Yes," she said, pulling away. "It's just a scratch."

There was an awkward pause.

Jonesy coughed. "What's the problem with the car?"

"See for yourself."

He circled round the front. "I see your problem alright. You've got a bloody great big roo sticking out of the windscreen."

"Hah, hah. Your powers of observation astound me," Em said. She shrugged. "It just jumped out in front of me.

"Can you get it going again?" she asked.

Jonesy surveyed the bonnet and the damage. He extracted the roo, lifting it to one side of the road, before brushing fragments of broken glass from his clothes. "Judging by the liquid pouring out, you've cracked your radiator and God knows what else." He wiped his hands. "We won't get it going any time soon. I could tow you back to the Visitors Centre?"

A Labrador sprung from the rear of the SUV and came bounding up to Jonesy, wagging its tail, it stood on its hind legs, trying to lick him.

"Lyra, how you going girl?" said Jonesy, scratching the dog under the chin. He'd missed the dog since the split with Em.

"I need to get info to headquarters at Ulambi ASAP, Jonesy. We've made a breakthrough at the observatory. I wouldn't have risked the storm last night otherwise."

"What do you mean?"

She opened the passenger-side door and fished around in her handbag before producing an external drive.

Jonesy scratched his head. "What's on that?"

"A recording," Em said.

"Of what?"

"You wouldn't believe me if I told you."

"Go-on. Try me."

"It's a recording of a non-earthed-based signal—possible proof of extrasolar life."

He snorted. "Bullshit. You mean to tell me you've got ET talking on that thing."

"Not talking, smartarse. It's a radio signal. This one appears not to have come from Earth. It will need to be substantiated of course. But, who knows? It could be aliens trying to send a message or an interstellar S.O.S. This could be huge."

"I don't know, Em." Jonesy sighed. "We should get you back to the Visitor's Center, and you should get that scratch—"

Lyra growled. Her hackles were up.

Jonesy observed the tree line, and the near impenetrable bushland beyond. Eucalypts swayed in an easy wind and cicadas buzzed. His skin crawled and he couldn't shake the feeling they were being watched.

Just then, he made out the faint outline of a figure, a shadow standing between the trees. *Is that a person?* But then it faded into the background, as quickly as it had appeared.

Lyra barked. There was a rustling from the bushes and a single emu stepped onto the track moving quickly, followed by another, and another.

*Strange.* It was like some kind of mass migration, he thought. Perhaps caused by the storm—or did it have something to do with Em's radio signal?

He shook his head.

"Arr, Jonesy, I think we should—"

"Leave? Yeah, I was thinking the same thing."

*** 

The Park Ranger's Office and Visitors Center was a simple, long brick building, with a corrugated tin roof. One half of the building was a shop for tourists while the other half was the ranger's office. As they pulled up, a wiry, Aboriginal man in a ranger's uniform came out to greet them.

"G'day, Em," the man said, as they stepped from the jeep.

She nodded. "Dazza."

"It's good to see you two together again."

"Pull your head in, Daz," Jonesy said.

Daz smirked.

The Labrador exited the jeep, barking and pawing at him.

"Cute dog," he said, "What's its name?"

"Lyra," Em said.

"She yours?" asked Dazza.

Em nodded.

"Well, you best come in then. We'll call the towing company at Ulambi. They'll get your car out. I've just put the kettle on."


The Park Rangers Office was confined but cozy. There was a desktop computer surrounded by a mess of papers, an ancient CB radio in the corner, and a giant map of the park pinned on a corkboard.

"I can't get through," Jonesy said, grimacing. I keep getting the engaged signal," He hung up the phone. "The lines must be down due to the storm."

Dazza put out a bowl of water for Lyra, as well as a leftover meat pie on a plate. She gobbled it with gusto.

"What happened to you?" he asked, gesturing to the scratch on Em's forehead, handing her a cup of tea he'd just poured.

"She hit a Roo on Cedar Creek Road," Jonesy said.

Dazza swore. Raising an eyebrow. "What were you doing out there?"

Em told him the events of that morning, including the strange behavior of some of the local wildlife.

"Let's hear that radio signal then," Jonesy said.

Em plugged the external drive into the computer and hit play. A loud sound emitted from the speakers.

"TCHK TCHK KHLAK, TCHK TCHK KHLAK, TCHK TCHK KHLAK…"

It was a peculiar sound, tremulous and distorted. It made the hair on Jonesy's arms stand up.

Dazza sat back and blinked.

"What's the matter, mate," Jonesy said. "Don't you believe in aliens?"

"You'd be surprised what I believe in."

Changing the subject he looked at Em. "You're lucky you're okay."

"She's fine, but her car is cactus," Jonesy said.

"No worries. We'll try the towing company again once the phone is back and working."

There came a burst of static and a voice over the CB radio. Dazza stood and picked up the receiver. "Hang on a sec," he said after a quick back-and-forth. He turned to Jonesy. "Hey, you were with that school group this morning?"

"Yeah."

"Where'd you see them last?"

"Banksia Ridge. Why?"

Dazza frowned. "They were supposed to head back to Ulambi. Their coach driver's saying they're a no-show."

Jonesy's heart sank. He joined Dazza by the radio. *What do you mean they didn't show?* he thought. *Shit. They'll be okay. They had their teacher with them.*

"They could be at Banksia Ridge picnic spot still," Dazza said over the radio. "We'll head over and take a look. Call us on the radio again if they turn up. Over."

"What's the matter?" asked Em, sensing the tone of the room had changed.

"A school group hasn't shown for their coach," Jonesy said, with hands on hips.

Dazza took the map from the corkboard and spread it out on the table. "Remind me where that picnic spot is again?"

Jonesy pointed.

"That's near Halls Gap," Dazza said.

Jonesy shrugged. "So?"

"It's where those German backpackers went missing last year." Dazza rubbed his lips in thought.

"Maybe we should go check on those kids?" Jonesy said.

*****

It was the middle of the afternoon by the time they reached Banksia Ridge; a small clearing with just a few weatherworn tables and benches, surrounded by dense bush and scrub. Tall gums stood around the clearing like lofty sentinels, the air fragrant with eucalyptus. Afternoon sun shone through the mantle of green, casting dappled patterns on the leaf-littered ground.

The school group was nowhere to be seen.

"Let's spread out," Jonesy said, walking the perimeter. He almost wished they'd brought the dog. *Perhaps she could have picked up on their scent?* He adjusted the shoulder straps of the rucksack he'd brought, containing a torch and a few other essential items.

"Cooeee!" cried Dazza, cupping his hands to his mouth, using the old bushman's call. His voice carried through the valley, resounding again and again, startling a flock of Sulphur-crested Cockatoos from their perch, resulting in a cacophonous—*Ree-reee-reee.*

"Where could those kids have gone?" Em said.

"They've got their teacher with them," Jonesy said, more so to reassure himself. *They'll be fine.* More than anyone he felt responsible for those kids.

"Oi, guys! Over here," Dazza said. He had been walking in a grid pattern before kneeling.

"You found something?" asked Em.

He handed it to her.

Em turned it over in her palm. A butterfly hair clip.

"I've seen that before," Jonesy said. "This morning. One of the kids—"

Dazza stood up. "You can see their tracks all around."

"Well, where are they now?" asked Jonesy.

"That's the million dollar question innit, mate?"

"They can't just have vanished."

Em screamed a high-pitched and blood-curdling scream, shattering the relative calm and setting her companion's teeth on edge.

Jonesy and Dazz jumped. "Are you okay?" they asked in unison.

"There's something in the trees," she said, in a shaky voice.

"I don't see —"

There came a strange whooping sound, unlike anything Jonesy had ever heard. It started low then rose sharply in pitch. He became aware of two figures, partially hidden by the trees, silhouette-like entities with large almond-shaped,eyes, watching.

Jonesy gasped and shuffled back a step. But the things vanished.

"Bloody hell!" Dazza said. "Did you see that?"

"Wh-what were they?" Em exclaimed. "You ever seen anything like that?"

Jonesy swallowed. "I might have," he said, thinking back to earlier in the day. "When I met you on Cedar Creek Road."

"Are you serious?" Em raised an eyebrow. "And you didn't say something?"

"I thought I'd imagined it."

Dazza laughed a nervous laugh. "I can't believe they're real."

Em and Jonesy wore blank expressions.

"Shadow men." Dazza shrugged. "I saw a doco about them on the SyFy channel. They're grey-skinned men, shadowy figures, 7 foot tall monsters — if you believe in such things. Every culture has a version of them. They look sort of human but definitely aren't. They live among the trees and rocks, following lost travelers, waiting until they let their guard down before snatching them away."

"Do you expect us to believe a bunch of boogeymen are on the loose *here* in Warrundella?" Jonesy said.

"Believe what you want, mate. I only know what I saw."

Em breathed in sharply. "You don't suppose those things took the kids, do you?

"Could be?" Dazza tilted his head. "I didn't want to say anything, but it looks like the tracks are headed towards Hart's Gap."

Jonesy looked in that direction.

"Is that bad?" Em asked.

Dazza huffed. "Hart's Gap is a large gorge, a focal point, a place of power. Locals have spoken about it, in whispered tones, for years. William Hart, the white explorer, went there in 1873, but his camels refused to enter the gorge, or to drink the water. It's just as mysterious as any Roswell or Area 51 if you ask me."

"What should we do?" Em asked.

"We're going to find those kids," Jonesy said.

***

The trio followed the missing school group's tracks along a rocky bush trail, calling for them all the while. The path took them higher and higher up the mountain. Progress was slow but eventually, the path led them through a narrow pass enclosed on either side by sheer limestone, and terminating at the mouth of a cave.

"What would've possessed them to go through there?" Em said.

"That's where their tracks lead," Dazza said.

A draft of dank musty air issued from the belly of the cave.

Jonesy produced the torch from his rucksack, and Em looked at him quizzically. He shrugged. "It pays to be prepared. Mind your step," he said, leading the way.

Darkness enveloped them, their footfalls echoing on the cavern floor.

After a while, they passed from a long corridor into a large cavern, where primitive rock art adorned the cave walls. There were a series of petroglyphs depicting stick figures with spears, scenes of hunting and gathering, and camp life.

"You recognize these, Dazza?" Jonesy asked.

"Nah, mate. They're not my mob. I've never seen anything like these."

Em ran her hands over the rock art, looking at them with wide eyes. "They must be tens of thousands of years old."

Jonesy examined a set of drawings depicting tribespersons kneeling before a giant rock monolith; flanked on either side by several elongated figures with strange dish-like eyes. "These look like the things we saw at the picnic site."

Em nodded. "And what about this one?" She pointed at a large blob-like shape.

Dazza shrugged. Glancing around he said, "This is a bad place."

There came a loud mewling noise followed by a high-pitched whoop.

Jonesy swore.

"Sounds like one of those things," Em said, in a shaky voice. "Did they follow us?"

"Let's go," Dazza said. "This place gives me the creeps."

They blundered their way into a smaller cavern where stalactites hung from the ceiling. The air was close and Jonesy could hear his own laboured breaths.

Another whooping call, then more whoops sounding in unison, chorusing.

They looked around frantically, trying to pinpoint the source.

"They're stalking us," Jonesy said. He shone his torch and they glimpsed a pair of red, glowing eyes.

Em screamed, gripping Jonesy's arm.

The trio retreated.

Dazza picked up a rock and hefted it in his hand.

One of the creatures stepped from the shadows, grabbing at Em and she shrieked. Jonesy stepped between her and the creature, the torchlight revealing its intimidating height and greyish skin.

"Piss off!" hissed Dazza, striking at it with the rock.

But more of the creatures pressed in, crowding and jostling. Dazza yelped as they latched onto him. Hooking their long arms under each of his armpits, they dragged him, kicking and screaming, into the dark.

"No!" Jonesy cried, laying into them with kicks and punches. But they easily repelled him, before retreating, dissipating like the ebbing tide.

Jonesy and Em were suddenly very alone. She wept uncontrollably.

"Fuck!" hissed Jonesy, veins standing out on his neck. He couldn't believe what had just happened. Things had gone terribly wrong. First the kids and now Dazza, he thought. *This has to be a dream.*

Jonesy ran a hand through his hair. His head was pounding and his chest ached. Dazza, his best mate, was gone, taken, or possibly dead. How could he come to terms with that? he thought. He needed a plan. He needed to move forward. *Pull yourself together.*

Placing a hand on Em's shoulder, he said, "We have to keep going."

Eventually, they exited the cave and found themselves in Harts Gap, a large gorge, with a stone-littered, clay floor, jagged rock formations, and surrounded by ancient, uniform red-brown cliffs.

Jonesy stared vacantly. He was still reeling from the loss of his friend.

A feeling of disquiet crept over them as the purple-hued sky gave way to the veil of night, and a myriad of stars sparkled in a sea of infinite dark.

"What about Dazza?" Em said. "We have to get help."

Jonesy unhitched the radio from his belt, switching it to an emergency channel.

*Kish*—"Hello? Mayday. This is Ranger Luke Jones with Doctor Emma Price. We're in trouble and need help. We're at Harts Gap. Is anybody there?" He paused for a response but all they heard was static. He tried several more times, switching channels, but again there was only static. "Shit!" he said, putting the radio away. "These cliffs must be blocking the signal."

"We can't stay here," Em said.

"And we can't go back," Jonesy said, looking in the direction of the cave. He clenched his fists. "C'mon, follow me. There has to be more than one way out of this gorge."

A short while later, on a clay mound, in the deepest part of the gorge, they found a giant rock monolith, 30 feet high and 10ft at its base. It seemed to defy gravity and the very air around it seemed electric. It gave Jonesy gooseflesh.

"I don't like this," Em said. "I think we should—"

Just then a dozen of the shadow men sprung forward, swarming over the rocks towards them, whooping and clawing. Jonesy and Em fought back but were quickly overwhelmed, as there were too many.

Jonesy's head was struck and he was momentarily dazed. They were dragged before the monolith and made to kneel. Looking up, he saw the clouds in the night sky quickly coalesce, and torrential rain began to pour in great heavy sheets.

One of the creatures moved forward, holding something out to him. Jonesy blinked, his eyes blurry from the rainwater. He realized it was Dazza's bloody and severed head. His deceased friend's dead eyes stared mournfully at the heavens.

"You bastards!" Jonesy screamed, trying to resist but was forced back down.

The tall, grey-skinned humanoid seemed amused. It turned and inscribed a set of bloody symbols on the monolith, before tossing the head.

The rain continued to pour.

"Jonesy?" Em said, in a shaky voice.

Loose stones levitated from the ground. Strange and incandescent colors danced and flashed, arcing outwards. The gorge echoed with thunder.

Something moved there in the dark; an immense shape, both colossal and nightmarish. It moved forth from the monolith, with great singleness of purpose.

Jonesy gasped, trying to look away.

Meanwhile, the shadow men whooped and gibbered.

It was a hideous, amorphous mass without recognizable limb or feature. If it resembled anything, it might have resembled a giant amoeba, thought Jonesy. Its gelatinous sides puffed in and out, rhythmically, in rasping breaths. Then, it made a deafening sound…

"TCHK! TCHK! KHLAK!"

Em screamed a shrill, ear-shattering scream.

"Don't look at it," Jonesy shouted, his heart beating faster and faster. He was sure he would go insane. Every moment ticked by slowly, like a lifetime.

A long sinuous tendril shot out from the creature, grabbing hold of Em.

"No. Take me!" yelled Jonesy, still restrained by the shadow men.

Em recoiled as the dreadful giant drew her near.

An aperture opened in its glistening, protoplasmic body, and it bit down. Em's head separated from her torso, and her lower half jittered on the blood-covered, ground.

Jonesy wailed, shaking uncontrollably, beside himself with grief. His cries were soon strangled, though. He could feel the creature's gaze and it looked right through his very soul. He felt a quickening and fell forward on his hands. Spasms wracked his body, and bone reformed. His arms grew long and spindly, and his skin turned grey. *I'm changing.* His thoughts lost all cohesion. A fresh bolt of pain, and the next sounds from his mouth were unrecognizable. He whooped and gibbered, a plaintive song to a storm ridden sky.

# Howl

Doyle was tired. His back and legs ached. They'd been hiking through dense jungle that whole morning, his skin covered with sweat and a profusion of tiny scratches. The air was suffocatingly hot and pungent with the scent of rotting vegetation. Dead leaves littered the forest trail, and forest vines threatened to ensnare.

He swore, and swatted a mosquito the size of a Dunstable lark. Was everything on the island so prodigious? Even the plant-life seemed unnaturally tall.

Ahead were his two travel companions. Bush as always was in the lead, using a sharpened piece of driftwood as a walking stick. A squat man, with a ruddy complexion, he was all brawn, and prone to outbursts of violence—as Doyle knew, painfully, from personal experience, having had run-ins with the sailor on more than one occasion.

Followed close behind by Clayton, who was Bush's opposite, in physicality and temperament. Clayton was tall and proud-looking. He was intelligent, even-tempered, and even though he was the more *senior* sailor, he knew better than to argue the point with the hotheaded Bush.

"Slow up," Clayton said. "Doyle's exhausted."

"Are you his governess?" Bush said. "Let him try and keep up."

Clayton looked back. "Sorry, old chap."

"Don't mention it," Doyle said, wiping his brow.

The three men had washed ashore, the sole survivors of the *Merry Gallant*—a merchant ship chartered by the British East India Company. She had been an old ship with unsound timbers, that foundered in a storm off the coast of West Africa; disappearing into the murky depths along with the rest of her thirty-six crew.

Doyle took out his father's pocket watch—his only possession to have made it off the ship, other than the rag-like clothes on his back. The watch's face was broken, but he could still make out his mother's portrait on the inner.

"Tell me again why we didn't stay on the beach?" Doyle asked.

"Food and fresh water," Bush called back.

Doyle put the watch away, his stomach rumbling at the mere mention of food.

"God will provide," Clayton said. "We just need to have faith,"

Bush laughed. "God helps those who help themselves."

"Do you honestly think you're going to kill anything with that piece of driftwood?" asked Clayton.

"Wait and see," Bush said, an almost gleeful look in his eye.

Clayton frowned. "I don't like bloodshed, Mr. Bush. All life has value."

Bush whirled around. "Why you pigeon-livered hypocrite—"

"Now, gentlemen, can't we change the subject?" Doyle said, stepping between them.

Bush's eyes narrowed, the vein standing out in his temple.

"It's a sin to be so enraged," Clayton said, coolly.

Bush snorted. "I look forward to being rescued, Clayton. I can do without your Bible-quoting and Quaker ways."

There came a snuffling sound, accompanied by the rustling of vegetation, like rooting around on the forest floor.

Bush shushed them, raising his hand.

They listened intently

He crept forward, brushing aside a palm frond, and there in front of them was a wild boar, full of vitality and covered with coarse hair; no more than a young hog, but, oddly, the size of a large Mastiff.

It was oblivious to them, concentrating on foraging.

Doyle imagined it on a spit above their campfire back on the beach. The meat could feed them for a week. They would have to be careful, though, as a couple of mean-looking tusks protruded from its jaws. It wouldn't do to get gored.

Another large insect whirred through the air.

Clayton moved, a twig snapping underfoot.

The boar reacted to the sound, its body alert.

Bush lunged forward with his sharpened stick, stabbing the boar in its side.

The boar squealed and tried to dash away.

It was too quick for Doyle, slipping his grasp.

Clayton dove for its hind legs, tackling the beast, clinging on, awkwardly.

Bush manoeuvred and stabbed the creature, over and over.

The sound of it dying reminded Doyle of a crying baby and the sight of the blood made him queasy. But he was hungry. Damn, he was hungry.

"There—I told you," Bush said, bent over double from exertion after the beast had fallen still.

Clayton chuckled, breathless.

"What a stroke of luck," Doyle said, grinning.

The three men started laughing in earnest; out of joy, relief, and triumph over their successful hunt.

"Now, we've just got to carry the bloody thing," Bush said.

Suddenly, there came a long and aggressive howl, and it rang through the forest, resonating with an eerie quality. It turned Doyle's blood cold and made his hair stand on end. It was unlike any animal or beast he'd ever heard.

All other forest noise fell silent.

The trio looked at each other, bewildered.

Bush hefted his stick.

The forest was moving. Something was in the underbrush and it was moving fast.

Doyle's stomach churned and his legs tightened, unsure whether to stand or run.

*Too late.*

A flurry of dark shapes sprung from the foliage, a horde of giant apes, screaming and drumming their chests. Doyle never knew such creatures existed in all of God's creation. They were great hulking brutes. Alternating between walking on all fours and standing, they were each about six feet tall. Formidable. Terrifying.

They had some of the characteristics of chimpanzees, Doyle thought— having seen a sad specimen in a cage, in Boma, the previous year—but these were different, more robust.

Doyle's face was ashen. He counted nine of them, all hooting and panting, encircling the trio, edging closer. They were mostly young males— except for the largest one, which was older with grey hair all over.

*He must be the alpha.*

"Rah! Get out of here ya mangy pack of monkeys," yelled Bush.

The alpha looked at him with its strangely human-like face, then covetously at their recent kill, and roared. Its mouth opened wide to expose four long canines and sharp incisors.

"Back up," said Clayton warily. "We're in their territory."

"No, dammit," Bush said. "If these poxy sons of bitches want our kill they've got another thing coming."

The alpha huffed its chest.

"Yah! Get out of it ya damned beasts," Bush exclaimed, brandishing his stick at them.

The alpha glared at him with hate-filled eyes, then pounced, knocking aside Burns' stick, landing on him, pummeling and biting.

It all happened so quickly.

The other apes piled on in a bloodthirsty frenzy.

"Help, Doyle!" Clayton cried while trying to pry them off.

Doyle had frozen unable to move. He had weighed things and didn't like the odds. At the same time, he cursed himself as a coward.

The apes attacked with such ferocity their strength and power seemed to eclipse anything in the natural world.

Clayton recoiled, screaming, after one of the apes locked jaws on his hand, removing a couple of his fingers.

Bush kicked and screamed while the mass of apes bit at his lips, nose, and genitals. They tore off his hands and feet. Then there was a cracking of ribs followed by a ululating cry, as one of the apes held Bush's heart aloft.

Clayton stood, pained expression on his face, blood seeping from his mutilated hand, pale and shaking. He swore, and tore off a piece of his shirt, wrapping his wound. "Run!"

And the two men ran for their lives, not in the direction of the beach, as they would've liked, but deeper into the jungle.

Despite his injury, Clayton ran at a steady pace, and Doyle had a hard time keeping up due to the difference in their strides. They ran around trees and leapt over logs, looking back from time to time. Behind them, they heard the howls of the apes.

Doyle's heart hammered in his chest, one thought repeating itself over and over, in his mind—*Not safe. Not safe*—keeping time with the in and out cycle of his breaths.

They came to a shallow stream and crossed it, the dreadful, chorus of howls intensifying. The apes were close. Too close. Doyle knew they would have to do something soon or suffer the same fate as Bush.

He had stumbled through a thicket when he looked back and realised Clayton had stopped.

Clayton hissed, motioning for Doyle to follow his example, and began climbing a tree.

He used a loose grip, clamping the bough with his feet, almost falling a couple of times, before making it to the middle branches and resting in the fork of the tree. This was no small feat, considering his injury. Fear can be a great motivator.

Doyle followed suit, climbing his own tree, barely making it to the middle branches before their pursuers burst through the underbrush. The apes moved through the forest, *with purpose*, stopping now and then to listen, the alpha in the lead, coordinating.

From his hiding spot, Clayton made a shushing gesture with his good hand. He looked sickly, pale.

Doyle nodded, clamping a hand over his mouth to silence a whimper.

*Oh, Jesus. Christ, deliver me.*

The apes fanned out, gesturing to one another, expanding their search.

One sniffed the ground beneath Doyle's tree.

*Oh, God. Please, no.*

In a panic, Doyle took out his pocket watch and threw it. It landed amid shrubs, the sound distracting the beast.

After a while, the apes moved off, still patrolling, searching, the sound of their grunts and growls growing more distant.

The two men shimmied down out of their trees.

Clayton looked about ready to pass out.

They doubled back towards the beach, looking back now and then to make sure they weren't followed. They made it as far as the stream before they heard the apes again.

"Into the water," Clayton said. "They can't track us."

They made their way along the length of the stream, water up to their knees, until eventually, instinct told them to veer left up an embankment. Clayton stopped at the top to cover himself with dirt.

Doyle looked at him, confused.

"To mask our scent," Clayton said.

Catching on, Doyle, too, covered himself with dirt.

They followed a trail, until it narrowed, and the forest became darker. Doyle's legs ached, and his chest heaved. At the end of the trail was a depression with a fissure in the rock face.

Behind them, the howls of the apes grew louder and more insistent.

"Dammit, they're at the stream," Doyle said, looking about frantically.

"In here," Clayton said, and the two of them climbed inside a small cave, a hidden cavity in the rock face.

And in there they waited.

Night fell. The howls of the apes had faded, replaced by the general sounds of the jungle. It began to rain; that sort of heavy torrential rain one only experiences in the tropics. They waited and shivered in the cold and wet. Sleep was impossible.

Clayton was in a bad way, nodding in and out of consciousness.

*It doesn't feel real to experience this suffering*, thought Doyle.

A praying mantis balanced on a vine at the mouth of their cave. Doyle watched it catch and eat a beetle.

*Mother nature is cruel.*

When the morning came, and the rain let up, Doyle and Clayton emerged from their cave. A ray of light shone through the forest canopy like the finger of God. It might have been beautiful under any other circumstances.

"Coast looks clear," Clayton said, looking about.

No sooner did he speak these words did the troop of apes appear, like a host of avenging, rebel angels rising from perdition.

The alpha jumped on Clayton's back sinking its teeth into his shoulder. Then more and more piled on, ripping and tearing. They tore at his face and hands.

"You devils!" Doyle tried to save his friend but was struck and fell backward onto a log.

When he looked again, Clayton was dead and some of the young males were dragging the body away.

They were eating him.

The rest of the troop formed a semi-circle around Doyle. The grey-haired alpha stood upright, stretching itself to its full intimidating height. It looked down on Doyle huffing its chest, a psychotic look in its eye.

Doyle felt the pulse in his temples and the blood in his veins surging like a current. An animalistic cry welled in him, escaping through his mouth.

"Bastard!" he screamed, picking up the log, launching himself at the alpha.

It howled ferociously in return and sprang to meet him.

Overcome with rage, and seeing the world through a red veil of hate, Doyle wanted only to destroy his enemy. Something shifted in him. He teetered on the precipice of insanity, before letting go, falling with abandon. It was unnatural and depraved, yet he experienced a lightness and a freedom he'd never before encountered. It was an awakening, a transformation. He felt younger, powerful.

Doyle bludgeoned the alpha, beating it about the head, repeatedly, until it fell unconscious, its skull exploding with a crunch of bone and a splatter of brains.

He fell back, hyperventilating, unsure what had come over him. He'd lost control and was covered with blood, his hands stained with blood. So much blood.

Realising their leader was dead, the other apes went quiet. They appeared unsure.

"Go away!" Doyle yelled.

Unperturbed, they crept forward, bowing low, submissive, each in turn gently touching the back of his hand. They were showing respect, electing him their new leader, their alpha.

Doyle could only manage a sick-sounding laugh. He wasn't well. Not at all. This wasn't the correct response.

But then his laughter turned to tears. With red rings under his eyes, he gazed up at the forest canopy. God's light had been extinguished. He was eternally lost. Forsaken.

The apes lingered for a time, before disappearing back into the forest, leaving Doyle to his malaise.

Doyle rocked back and forth. He had forgotten who he was, lost in his own world of madness and despair. The fire of his rage still burning bright, he tilted back his head and let out a long and tortured howl.

# Moist

I pulled up in my battered Saab, and peered through the windscreen. The old lakehouse stood solemnly, in the Victorian style, with steeply pitched towers and gables. It had belonged to my uncle Felix, a former professor of entomology—deceased. In retrospect, there was something off about the place—not just the usual decay of an old house, but a stillness. Rain pattered, interrupting the smooth surface of the lake. Willows lined the shore, their drooping branches twisted like gnarled hands, cloaked in shrouds of green.

Buster, my Labrador Retriever, let out a bark—an overgrown pup with boundless energy and a heart of gold, he was as loyal and steadfast as they come.

"I know, boy," I said, scratching behind his ear. It's not the Ritz, but it will have to do—C'mon. Let's get familiar with our new home."

The realtor was already there, his Lexus parked to one side.

I opened the car door, donned my raincoat, and grabbed my box of things from the backseat. It had started to rain more in earnest, and my loafers were buried halfway up to their tassels in the mud. I danced across the muddy puddles and sprang up the stairs to the porch.

"You found it!" The realtor grinned. "Hector Kasabian," he said, extending his hand.

"Ryan Lucan," I said, as I shook it, balancing the box on one knee.

The roof over the porch leaked in several places. I shuffled my feet, and my socks, which had been soaked through, squelched uncomfortably in my shoes. Buster panted beside me, his breath visible in the cool, damp air.

Hector jangled the keys. "We kept the place as your uncle, Felix, left it—Shall we go in and take a look?"

"Sure," I said.

"Don't you need to grab the rest of your things first?" he asked.

My face flushed red. "This is it," referring to the box.

Hector raised an eyebrow.

I shrugged. "I travel light."

Inside, I put the box down and removed my raincoat.

Hector felt along the wall until he found the light switch, and a multitude of bulbs came on. The light revealed we were in a large foyer area with timber floors.

"What do you think?" he said.

I wrinkled my nose. "It smells a bit fusty."

He sniffed. "Aw, don't worry about that. All the houses in Willow's Hollow smell like this. Comes with living near the lake. Seriously—just open the windows on a sunny day, let the breeze roll through, and before you know it, she'll smell like fresh biscuits riding a unicorn."

I chuckled, scanning the foyer. "What's this?" I asked, pointing to a black mark on the wall.

Hector slipped on his glasses and stepped closer.

"That's rising damp," I said.

He grimaced. "You still sure you want to live here? I mean… you don't want to sell? I could help you flip it."

I shook my head. "This'll do."

Buster barked—loud and sudden—his eyes locked on the wall.

*Odd.*

I gave him a reassuring pat.

"I plan to stay a while… do the restorations. What was good enough for my uncle is good enough for me."

***

I set the box down in the kitchen and began unpacking. Among my things: Buster's bowl and leash, a bag of TallyWag dog treats, a sleeping bag, a box of Choco Crunch, a gallon of milk, a jar of instant coffee, a six-pack of beer, and my laptop— brought along in the vague hope I'd finally finish my novel, *The Big Easy*, a gritty noir about a hard-boiled private eye in 1940s New Orleans.

"Home sweet home, hey, boy?" I said.

Buster tilted his head.

I set his bowl down and gave him a treat.

The kitchen was galley-style, with a cold stone floor, an ancient stove, a vintage fridge with chrome handles, and a walk-in pantry stocked with rows of canned goods—beans, diced fruit, pickles, sardines—and a plastic tub filled to the brim with salt.

I scratched my head. "Why so much salt, Uncle? Didn't anyone tell you it's bad for your blood pressure?"

I grabbed the kettle from the stove, went to the sink, and turned the faucet. The pipes groaned, then spat out a violent burst of stained water.

"Dammit," I muttered. "That's all I need—a plumbing problem." I sighed and dropped the kettle in the sink.

I grabbed one of the lukewarm beers, popped the ring pull, and took a quick sip to keep the foam from overflowing.

Buster looked at me and licked his chops.

"Oh, alright." I poured some into his bowl, and he lapped it up enthusiastically.

Once he was done, we moved on to explore the rest of the house.

In the foyer, I made another mental note about the rising damp and the spreading mold. The place had the scent of long-term neglect.

The parlor was somewhere between a library and a taxidermy exhibit. Mint green wallpaper peeled at the corners beneath a high, shadowed ceiling. A stuffed crow and an owl kept watch from opposite shelves, while rows of leather-bound books lined the walls. Between them, glass display cases held pinned insect specimens—moths, grasshoppers, beetles— everything from massive stag and rhino beetles out of Australia to delicate butterflies like the monarch and blue morpho.

I imagined them fluttering in their death throes as the pins went in. The thought made my skin crawl.

At the center of it all stood Uncle Felix's desk, buried under books and papers in precarious, teetering stacks. Felix had always been intensely curious—and mildly obsessive.

"Messiness is a sign of industry," he used to say.

Atop one pile sat his field notebook—the one he carried everywhere. The leather cover was cracked and split at the spine. The pages were warped, blotched with reddish fungal blooms, and faintly sticky to the touch. His meticulous sketches filled the pages—leaf beetles, fungal colonies—annotated with GPS coordinates, Latin species names, and observations in his tight, precise handwriting.

Some pages were torn, others singed or missing. A few were fused together with a resin-like substance I couldn't identify.

It felt like a map of his mind: fragmented, intense, and strangely beautiful.

"Alright, old man," I muttered, flipping through. "Let's see what you were working on."

Zoological terms filled the margins.

*Field Journal - June 11th, Dusk - Edge of Chanchamayo Valley*
*Weather: humid, high-70s, light mist settling over moss beds*
*Specimen Focus: Terrestrial Gastropoda (assorted Pulmonata)*

*Observed a slug working its way up the damp root of a kapok tree. They're slow, yes—but hunger gives them an uncanny will. I've noted more than once these soft-bodied creatures turning carnivorous when conditions are lean. Carrion, eggs, even other snails—the line between herbivore and scavenger blurs when the hunger's deep enough. No teeth in the way a predator has teeth, but that radula—thousands of microscopic hooks, scraping—*

*— Dr. Felix Lucan, entomologist*

"What even is this?" I sighed, shaking my head, and set the field guide down. "Just say it like it is—'Slug was slow. Ate stuff.' Done. Could've saved a whole page." It was late, and I figured it was time to call it a night.

Upstairs, in the bedroom, the floorboards groaned with every step. Dust clung to everything, and spiderwebs draped across forgotten furniture. I found an old four-poster bed beneath thick, heavy curtains. No one had stayed there in ages.

"Well, this is home for the night," I said to Buster. "Just you and me, ace."

I tossed down my sleeping bag, kicked off my shoes and socks, and flopped face-first onto the mattress—completely wiped.

***

I awoke, coughed, and turned over. Then—

*Click-click, scrape-scrape.*

I froze, ears straining. *What the hell was that?* I peered into the darkness, but saw nothing. Reaching for the phone on the nightstand, I tapped the screen. 00:00 Midnight.

*Click-click. Scrape-scrape.*

*There it is again. A noise. Inside the wall? What is that?*

I peered again into the stygian blackness of the room, but saw nothing. I couldn't pinpoint the source of the noise. It was a strange, intermittent scuffling.

*Weird. A raccoon in the wall, maybe?*

But just as suddenly as it came, the sound stopped. Instead, I heard Buster, snoring beside me. He didn't stir. "Some guard dog you are," I muttered.

I rolled out of bed. The air was thick, stifling. I shuffled across the room and opened a window. The rain had lightened, a misty drizzle now. The window frame groaned—the latch was broken, and the wood was soft with rot.

I sighed. "Great. Another thing I have to fix."

Barefoot, I padded across the worn-out carpet and down the stairs, phone light in hand. Just as I reached the bottom, the phone died. I couldn't find the wall switch in the dark.

*You've got to be kidding me.*

In the kitchen, I fumbled for a glass in the cupboard. My mouth was dry and gummy. I was desperate for water, so I turned the faucet. Again, the pipes rattled and hammered.

*Right. No water. Forgot about that. Maybe it had been the pipes making noise in the walls?*

Giving up, I went to the fridge and grabbed a beer. But just as I shifted my weight—*Squish*—something burst under my foot. *Wet. Slime.*

"What the—?"

I stepped again and—*Squish. Pop.*

"Christ!"

Opening the fridge wider, the dull yellow light spread across the stone floor.

*SLUGS!*

A semicircle of them surrounded me. They were gray-green or orange with leopard-like spots. They wriggled. Squirming. Sliding.

"Fuck! Jesus—Eew!"

I tried to back up, but—*pop*—another one.

I bolted for the bathroom. Flipped the light switch. Sat on the edge of the tub and lifted my foot. Slime clung to the sole, thick as jelly.

I turned the faucet—More stained, discolored water. It reeked.

"Shit!"

I grabbed a hand towel, trying to wipe the goop away, but succeeded only in smearing the sticky, stubborn mucus—like some kind of glue.

I cracked the beer, took a long drink, then poured the rest over my foot, trying not to gag as I imagined the slug's innards turned to paste.

I scrubbed again with the towel. It helped, but barely.

Then came the sound of claws on tile. Buster, awake now, nosed the bathroom door.

"Don't look at me like that," I said. "You weren't there."

Afterwards, I used another towel to scoop up the slugs and dumped them into an old ice cream tub from the pantry. I went outside barefoot, into the rain, and hurled the little bastards into the bushes.

"Fuck you!" I shouted. "I hope you get eaten by birds!"

I went back inside, dripping from the rain.

Buster met me at the bottom of the stairs.

"That's it. I'm calling a plumber in the morning," I muttered, flicking off the kitchen light. "And a pest guy."

Buster panted.

I pointed at him. "Remind me."

***

The next morning dawned bright and clear, the sky a brilliant blue. I took Buster for a walk along the lake's edge. Nose to the ground, tail wagging, he trotted ahead—head down, bum up—sniffing at everything in sight. I found a piece of driftwood and tossed it. He bounded after it, delighted. Overhead, a flock of geese passed in a perfect V-formation, flying south for the winter. Along the shore, the willows loomed like sentinels from another world, their limbs swaying as the wind whispered through them, casting a quiet melancholy over the scene.

Later, I drove into town in the old Saab to pick up a few supplies—but not before following Hector's advice: I opened all the windows to let the house breathe. I wasn't too concerned about security. Willow's Hollow was remote, almost suspended in time—the kind of place where people still left their doors unlocked. And really, what was there to steal? Uncle Felix's books? My small box of belongings?

Willow's Hollow was your typical whistle-stop, semi-rural town, wedged between forest and farmland. Main Street had all the essentials: a town hall, a school, and a handful of dusty storefronts—a general store, a hardware store, an old theatre, and *Whiskey Business,* the only bar in town and proud of its terrible name.

I tied Buster's leash to a nearby bike rack—he panted, scratched behind his ear, then flopped onto the pavement with a sigh. Inside the general store, I grabbed a few groceries and a pack of bottled water—I'd need it for coffee. I can't function without coffee. After loading the bags into the Saab, I headed to the hardware store and picked up paintbrushes, rubber gloves, a mask, chemical mold remover, and a couple of electric fans.

On my way back, I ran into Hector. He was out of his real estate uniform and had his twin daughters with him, arguing over whose turn it was to ride the coin-operated helicopter by the shopping carts.

"How was your first night in the lake house?" Hector asked.

"I've had better," I said, and launched into the story about the slugs.

"Ugh." Hector grimaced.

"Did Felix ever mention anything about slugs?"

He shook his head. "Although—"

The girls started bickering in the background.

"Girls! Knock it off," Hector said sharply.

They glanced at their father, subdued for a moment—then resumed their argument, just more quietly.

"I guess it's not that unusual, with the rain we had last night," Hector said. "Maybe they came in looking for somewhere warmer."

I nodded.

"What's all that stuff for?" Hector asked, nodding toward the fans and hardware supplies I was carrying.

"It's for the mold—the rising damp," I replied.

Hector looked impressed. "So, you're really going to try fixing the place up, huh? And I still can't convince you to sell?"

I shook my head.

"Anything I can do to help?"

Hector's girls were now petting Buster, who happily licked their hands, making them giggle.

"Well, actually… now that you mention it, do you know a good plumber?"

"Sure. Bit of an all-rounder, actually. In a place like Willow's Hollow, you've got to wear a few hats. It's Sunday, so he'll either be at church or down at Whiskey Business. I'll send him over tomorrow—he can give you a quote."

"That'd be great. Thanks."

"Come on, girls," Hector called. "Leave the man's dog alone."

Buster barked and wagged his tail as the girls dashed off, giggling.

On the walk back, I passed a gazebo tucked into the corner of the park. The weather was too nice to ignore, so after dropping off my things, I circled back and set up with my laptop and a bottle of Coke. I settled in and began tapping away—working on the novel. Buster stretched out beside me, resting his head on my leg. I scratched behind his ear. My eyes drifted back to the blinking cursor on the screen.

Then, suddenly, the words came...

CHAPTER 18
The Dame in the Smoke

There were footsteps in the hall outside the office—click clack, click clack.

The woman appeared from around the door. She was tall, beautiful, a knockout in a flower print dress. She strode across the office, a sparsely furnished room with a line of file cabinets along the wall, and a desk at its centre.

"Detective Boudreaux?" she asked. The light shone in the window. Her hair was color of spun gold, and her eyes were like jewels--opalescent and watchful.

"That's right," said the man sitting behind the desk. "I'm Jesse Boudreux." He had a rugged face, a wiry frame, and an air of vigilance. He took a cigarette from the soft pack on his desk and searched for a light.

"I wasn't sure," she said, gesturing towards the broken glass of the door, where normally the detective's name would have been. She studied him.

He struck a match and lit his cigarette.

"Celeste," she said, offering her hand. "Celeste Marquette."

Boudreax shook it, gesturing for her to sit. "What can I do for you, Miss Marquette?"

She kept her eyes fixed on him while fidgeting with her hands. This just went to show the woman's mental state.

"I heard you're good at finding things."

```
      He scoffed. "It's not my area of
expertise, but--"
      "I need a reliable detective. My
sister, Delilah, is missing."
      Jesse looked up, surprised. "Not
Delilah Marquette, the legendary jazz
singer?"--
```

My cell phone chirped. It was Jane.

I swallowed hard and picked up the phone.

"Hey," came her voice—warm, soft, unmistakably hers. Just hearing it was enough to make me falter, to want to forget everything and beg her to come back.

"Why are you calling?" I asked.

"C'mon, Ryan. Don't be like that. I'm just checking in. I'm worried about you."

"You lost that right when you slept with someone else."

"That doesn't mean I stopped caring," she said. "I still love you. Just... not the way you want. I want us to be friends, okay? I hate the thought of you alone in that old, rundown house."

"Well, that's where you're wrong." I glanced down. "I have Buster."

She sighed. "How is old Buster?"

I looked at him. He panted, tongue lolling. "He's good. He's been asking about you."

She chuckled softly. "So, how are you, Ryan? Really?"

I exhaled. "I'm fine."

"It's okay to ask for help if you need it," she said gently.

"I don't need a handout," I snapped. "How's old moneybags, anyway?"

"You know he hates it when you call him that."

"Sorry... Wade, then. How's Wade?"

There was a pause.

"I'm gonna go," she said. "I'm sensing some hostility."

"Look, I'm sorry, okay? It's just... it's hard."

"I know," she said quietly. "Take care, Ryan."

*Click.*


By the time I got back to the house, dusk had settled in. The windows were still open, so I made a quick lap through the place, shutting them before the night air crept in. I tossed the groceries into the fridge, then threw a steak on the pan. The kitchen filled with the smell of sizzling meat. I cracked a beer, poured a generous layer of A1 sauce on the steak, and ate while standing at the counter.

That night, while lying on the four-poster bed, the cold crept in as soon as the sun disappeared. Rain pattered on the roof tiles—soft at first, then building into a torrent. Thunder rumbled somewhere in the distance. I pulled Buster close, his warmth a comfort in the growing chill.

Then came the sound again—*click click, scrape scrape*—from inside the wall. It was like someone clumsily shifting furniture in the next room. The kind of sound that didn't belong. The kind that made a house feel haunted.

This time, Buster growled.

I held my breath and listened, but the noise faded.

Eventually, my eyelids grew heavy. As sleep pulled me under, I almost managed to convince myself it was just the storm.

***

The next morning, I set up shop in the foyer. I spread drop sheets across the floor and unpacked a few tools. With a scraper in hand, I began peeling away the bubbling paint from the walls—evidence of black mold caused by rising damp.

To my dismay, the deeper I scraped, the worse the damage became. Beneath the cracked surface, more mold festered, creeping like a dark stain beneath the plaster.

"We've got a real problem here, boy," I muttered to Buster, who sat nearby, watching with keen eyes.

I pulled on a pair of rubber gloves, zipped up my overalls, and strapped on a mask. Taking a paintbrush, I began applying a thick mold treatment solution to the worst patches.

The fumes soon overwhelmed me. The stale air trapped inside the mask made my head spin; I grew dizzy, on the verge of hyperventilating. I stepped back, steadied myself, and set up a few fans to circulate fresh air through the room.

Outside, rain drummed steadily against the roof. A slow leak had started again. I placed a bucket beneath the newest drip.

Suddenly, a sharp knock came at the door.

Buster barked furiously.

On the front stoop stood a man in grease-streaked overalls, his thick, Coke-bottle glasses catching the dull light. His head was crowned with a mop of gray hair.

"You must be the plumber," I said.

"Ayuh, reckon I am. Wouldn't be here otherwise," he grinned. "Name's Ray. Good to meet you. Hector Kasabian sent me—said you've been having some trouble with the pipes?"

I nodded. "You might as well come in."

Ray stepped inside, surveying the scene: the drop sheets, the fans, the scraped walls.

"You've been busy," he said.

"Mold," I replied. "Or, a plumbing issue. Not sure."

Ray nodded. "Let's take a look."

I led him to the kitchen, where discolored, stained water filled the sink, and the pipes rattled ominously whenever the faucet ran. Then I showed him the bathroom, where the same problem persisted.

"Yup," Ray said. "Something's backed up. Question is, where's it coming from? You got a basement?"


Down in the basement, I pulled a chain hanging from the ceiling, and a lone bulb flickered on. Buster waited at the top of the stairs, tail wagging like this was some kind of adventure.

The place smelled damp. Dust coated the narrow wooden steps. Shelves lined the walls, stacked with jars of pickled fruits and vegetables—most of them covered in cobwebs. Overhead, a web of pipes crisscrossed the low ceiling.

"What do you think?" I asked.

Ray, who'd come down behind me, pointed to a dark stain low on the concrete wall. "This right here? That's your problem spot. Water table's been high before. Happens all the time with lakehouses out here in Willow's Hollow."

I nodded. "Still doesn't explain why the pipes are blocked."

Ray shut off the mains. He climbed a ladder, pulled a screwdriver from his belt, and gave one of the pipes a few sharp taps. It thudded dully.

"Yup," he said. "She's blocked. There's your culprit."

He grabbed a monkey wrench and started loosening a joint in the pipe.

*SLOSH!*

A gush of black sludge poured out—and then came the slugs.

"Argh! Slugs!" Ray yelped, trying to backpedal. He flailed at the top of the ladder, one foot kicking out—and punched a hole clean through the drywall.

I barely managed to grab the ladder and steady him. Slugs were raining down. Wet. Slimy. *Plip, plop, plip.*

"Oops—sorry 'bout that," Ray said, grimacing. He pulled out a handkerchief and wiped black goo off his cheek. "I'll patch that."

I looked down, crushed a few slugs under my boot. "What the f—?"

"There's your explanation," Ray said, still catching his breath. "Slug infestation. It's rare, but it happens. They find their way into the plumbing—moist and dark, they love it in there."

"This is disgusting," I muttered.

"Leave it to me," Ray said. He headed back out to his truck and returned with a powered drain auger—long, flexible cable coiled like a snake.

"If this doesn't clear 'em out, nothing will."

Meanwhile, I needed to get clean. I asked what I should do.

Ray didn't skip a beat. "Go jump in the lake. Literally. Lotta folks do it around here. It's cold, but it'll wash the gunk off."

So I did. With Buster at my heels, I headed to the lakeshore, soap and towel under one arm.

*I hate slugs. Is there anything worse in the world? Why'd it have to be slugs?*

I left my towel and clothes beneath a willow tree, wearing only my briefs. Rain still fell, light but steady, and the cold, slick stones pressed sharply into my bare feet as I walked to the water's edge.

*Holy Moses, it was cold.*

I lasted ten minutes, tops. Skin goose-pimpled, teeth chattering. Buster stared at me from the shore like I'd lost my mind.

In the distance, I could still hear the auger whining from the house.

Then—

A scream.

I jumped out of the water, heart hammering. Buster barked, frantic. I grabbed my towel, wrapped it around me, and sprinted back to the house, water streaming down my legs.

Downstairs, the auger was still going. But Ray wasn't at the ladder.

He came bolting up the stairs instead, face pale, eyes wide.

"What happened?" I asked.

Ray was panting. "You're not gonna believe me. I was down there, clearing the pipe—more slugs come out, sure—but then I heard this... rumble in the wall. And I looked down..."

He held his hands out, indicating a wide arc.

"There's a slime trail down there. Big one. Glistening. Silvery. Thing's massive."

I frowned. "Bullshit."

"You callin' me a liar?" he said, clearly rattled. "I'm telling you, you got a big one down there."

I wrapped the towel tighter. "If you're right... what the hell am I supposed to do about it?"

Ray looked down at his boots. "Give me a minute. Pest control ain't exactly my specialty. But I got some stuff in the truck that might help."

***

So, while Ray got to work, I headed upstairs to get dressed. Then I made my way to the parlour and sat at the writing desk. I cleared a stack of books and papers to make space, then settled in and returned to my novel.

CHAPTER 21
The Blue Orchard

Boudreaux stepped into the Blue Orchid — a lush, smoky nightclub draped in velvet and thick with secrets. The kind of place where the drinks were expensive, the memories cheap, and nobody asked too many questions.

*I've gotta find Delilah,* he thought. *Celeste is paying good money, and I don't turn down good money.*

The club was soaked in red light and jazz. A trio played slow and low from the velvet-curtained stage. Dancers lounged on velvet chaises, legs crossed. Smoke curled like gossip in the lamplight.

The bar stretched the length of the back wall, polished dark wood with the gloss of too many spilled drinks. Behind it, shelves rose in neat, shimmering rows—colorful bottles lit from below, glowing like stained glass at a sinner's chapel.

The barman was a beefy man in his fifties, all forearms and suspicion, with a permanent scowl etched into his square jaw. He was drying a highball glass with a rag that looked like it had seen too many bad nights and not enough bleach.

"Glass of your finest regret, bartender," Boudreaux said, sliding onto a stool. "Something that burns on the way down."

The barman looked up. "Jesse Boudreaux," he said, not quite smiling. "Well, well. We haven't seen you here in a while. What kind of rock you been drinkin' under?"

Boudreaux smirked and leaned an elbow on the bar. "Been busy perfecting the art of disappointing women and evading creditors. Good to see you, Mickey. You still serving drinks, or just dishing out judgment?" He tapped the bar. "How 'bout a whiskey, neat—and maybe a name to go with it?"

Mickey's jaw tightened just a little—enough to notice—but he kept drying the glass, then poured two fingers of amber into a heavy tumbler and slid it across.

"Say," Boudreaux said casually, "just making conversation here...but you haven't seen Delilah Marquette around lately, have you?"

"Delilah who?" Mickey said too quickly, his eyes flicking sideways for just a beat.

I stopped writing for a moment. I could still hear Ray noisily working in the background, which made it hard to focus at first. But eventually, I settled back into the rhythm and picked up the thread of the story again.

Boudreaux took a sip of the whiskey--smoky, mean, and just the right kind of burn. He set the glass down and leaned forward, voice low.

"Now c'mon, Mickey. I know you're lying." He smiled without warmth. "Don't try to bullshit a bullshitter."

Mickey didn't blink.

"I know for a fact Delilah Marquette used to work here. She danced. Sang. Hell, she practically lit this place up. Now she's gone. Off the grid. And dollars to donuts, your boss Lucetti's got something to do with it."

That got a flicker out of Mickey-- the tiniest twitch of his upper lip. A

lot of things lived behind that face:
regret, loyalty, maybe even fear.

But before he could speak, a voice
cut in behind Boudreaux--smooth,
unhurried, and cold as steel.

"Get up."

Boudreaux stiffened. He felt the
unmistakable press of a gun muzzle
nestling between his shoulder blades.

"Turn around. Face the wall."

Looking out the window, I realized it was getting late. The sky had darkened more than I'd noticed. I hadn't heard from Ray in a while, so I decided to check on him.

The basement was dimly lit, the single bulb swaying gently from the ceiling.

"Ray?" I called.

Nothing.

Slugs glistened on the floor, weaving through streaks of black sludge. No sign of Ray—except for the motorized auger and his toolbelt, lying on the ground. It was slick with a glittery trail of slimy mucus.

"Ew. What the—?"

I turned and went outside. His truck was still there.

*Strange.* He wouldn't just leave without his truck or his toolbelt. *Maybe he got a phone call? An emergency?* I tried to come up with a reason. *But then... why would he leave everything behind? Maybe he went to Whiskey Business? Hector did say he liked the place...*

Heading back to the basement, I called, "Ray? Hey, Ray?" scratching my head.

Buster stood beside me and barked once, ears pricked.

"Where could he have gone?" I asked, mostly to myself.

I headed back into the basement. Something didn't feel right.

Then I saw them—legs, sticking out from behind the water heater.

*Seriously? Asleep on the job?*

"Hey, Ray?" I said, giving one boot a nudge.

His leg shifted slightly—limp.

No response.

I sighed. "This is no time to be dozing."

I stepped around the heater. And screamed—*"AHHH!"*—for there were Ray's legs partly chewed, and dismembered, lying in a pool of shimmering slime.

In that moment of panic, Buster yelped and bolted up the stairs.

"Buster! Come back! Buster!"

***

I sat stiffly in a hard plastic chair in the police waiting room, staring into nothing. The faint hum of fluorescent lights buzzed overhead. Somewhere behind the glass partition, a printer whirred, and an officer cleared his throat.

But I didn't move. I just sat there—shell-shocked, hands clenched, mind looping through the basement, the toolbelt, the slime. My heart lurched. Even with everything swirling in my mind, one thing stood out clearly: Buster was gone. He'd slipped away, and the thought of him out there alone, lost or scared, twisted the knot in my stomach tighter. I hoped he'd found a safe spot nearby, just waiting for me to catch up. Still, I knew I couldn't stay here long—I needed to find him.

The door opened with a creak. Hector stepped in, hesitating for a second before sitting beside him.

"Jesus," Hector muttered. "You look like hell."

I didn't answer right away. Finally, in a low voice: "I told them everything."

"And?"

"They said they'd send someone over to check. Like it was a welfare visit. No sense of urgency."

He gave a bitter laugh.

"Maybe I should've said it was a gas leak instead of a half-eaten plumber."

Hector didn't laugh.

A moment passed. I turned to him slowly. "Can you tell me about my uncle's death?"

Hector looked uncomfortable. "Why do you want to know about that?"

"Humor me."

He shrugged. "It was winter. Cold as hell. Your uncle may have had dementia, they think— undiagnosed?"

I shrugged. "Maybe."

Hector frowned. "Anyway, the story goes that Felix wandered outside in just a thin sweater, right in the middle of one of those thick lake mists—the kind where you can't see your own damn feet."

"And he just… died?"

"Exposure. Hypothermia. They found him under a willow tree, near the lake's edge. Must've gotten turned around in the fog. He lived alone, remember?"

"But why'd he need a closed casket?"

Hector rubbed the back of his neck. "Strange thing …by the time they found him, the body wasn't in good shape. Weather must have got to it…or something. His skin had already started to bloat. Already decomposing. Moist. "

I stared at the floor. "Did they… investigate?"

"They did the basics. Autopsy came back inconclusive, I think. Too decomposed. Official cause was listed as something like... cardiac arrest, due to advanced decomposition. Paperwork kind of brushed it aside."

I swallowed.

***

I wanted to leave, but couldn't—not without Buster. I searched for him, but it was no use. He was gone. All I could do was hope that one day I'd open the door and find him sitting on the front stoop, that dumb grin on his face like nothing had happened.

In the meantime, I had to stay busy—anything to keep my mind off it. I decided to take care of the plumbing repairs myself. With Ray gone now, I figured he wouldn't mind if I used his tools. I grabbed his old toolbelt and hauled the auger down to the basement.

I pulled up a YouTube tutorial—*"DIY Drain Snake for Homeowners."* The guy in the video was overly chipper. I tried to follow along.

Wrench in hand, I start unscrewing a pipe when—

*Click-click. Scrape-scrape.*
I froze. The sound came from behind the wall.

I looked up—and through a jagged hole in the drywall, I caught a glimpse of something. Massive. Wet. Moving.

"What the fuck is that?!"

Whatever it was, it slithered out of sight in a blur of flesh and a shimmer.

My tools clattered to the floor as I bolted up the stairs, heart hammering.

In the kitchen, my hands shook. My breath came in short, shallow bursts. My legs felt like they were filled with sand.

*I didn't believe Ray before—but I believe him now.*

And then it hit me—Buster was gone. The basement. That *thing*.

*What if it has Buster?* I swallow down a sob. "Shit."

I took out my phone and dialled Jane. She picked up on the second ring.

"Hey, you." Her voice was soft. Familiar. I nearly fell apart.

"Hey," I say, trying to keep it together. "Sorry to bother you. I just... I didn't know who else to call."

"What's going on? You okay?"

I hesitated. I couldn't tell her everything—not yet. She'd never believe me. And if she knew I'd lost Buster... it would destroy her.

"I'm just... kind of scared," I admit, voice low. "Weird noises in the basement. Weird day. Ray's gone—the plumber. And Buster's... missing."

There's a pause.

"Oh no. I'm so sorry. You want me to come over?"

"No. No—it's okay. I just... needed to hear your voice."

She was quiet for a second, then said gently, "You're not alone, okay? Whatever's going on, you'll get through it. I'm here."

My throat tightened. I press a hand to my chest, to keep my heart from punching through it.

"I love you," I whisper.

There was a long pause.

"I love you too," she said. "Now, please be careful."

"I will."

I hung up.

But the silence that followed felt heavier than before.

I glanced toward the basement door.

***

I paced the length of the parlor, back and forth, wearing a threadbare trail into the carpet. My hands shook, and my thoughts raced. Every few steps, I glanced toward the front door, then toward the basement, as if caught between running out and hiding. But I couldn't leave. Not without Buster.

He was out there somewhere. Lost. Alone. Maybe hurt.

The memory of the plumber—what was left of him— flashed in my mind. A giant slug? A slug, of all things? I didn't know something like it could exist outside of nightmares.

Now it lived in this house. In the walls. In the basement.

I stopped. My eyes darted towards my uncle's cluttered desk. A scattered mess of notes, clippings, and old scribbled maps.

Then I remember.

*The field journal!*

Without thinking, I shove everything off the desk with a loud thud—papers, books, a half-empty coffee mug. It all crashes to the floor.

I slam the worn leather-bound journal down in the cleared space and open it wide. The pages smell of damp paper and ink. I begin to read...

*Thursday, 22<sup>nd</sup> of August – I can't believe the expedition has finally begun. Today, we head deep into the wilds of the Peruvian Amazon. Our journey started with a flight to Pucallpa, where we boarded a boat that carried us down the Ucayali River—our* *gateway into the rainforest. From there, we transferred to a smaller vessel that took us deeper into the primary jungle. After a long trek on foot, we set up a field camp, surrounded by towering trees and the hum of life all around. Then came the real adventure: navigating the dense interior. We hacked our way through thick undergrowth with machetes, led by a local indigenous tracker named Chaska. The name couldn't have been more fitting—Chaska means "star" in his native Asháninka tongue. Chaska was slim and wiry, with dark eyes—like the night sky— that glinted, as if distant stars were watching from within.*

*Monday, 26th of August – Observed unusual slime patterns again—unusually large mucus trails, with bioluminescent residue near decomposing trunks. Suggests an unidentified gastropod, likely new genus. Possibly arboreal? Curiously patterned. Almost… deliberate? Spiraling trails glowing faintly under UV light. The viscosity is "heavier than banana slug excretion," and there is"faint acrid odor, like burning hair.*

*I consulted Chaska, our Peruvian guide. He said the slime belongs to a giant slug, to 'kamári'— some kind of forest spirit. Spiritual nonsense, of course, but the term intrigued me. He was hesitant to lead us further, spoke of curses, but I convinced him. Curiosity trumps myth.*

*We climbed for 3 days and 3 nights up Monte del Uraq Sombra, the Mountain of White Shadow. The canopy was nearly impenetrable. Humidity at 97%. Leeches inside our boots. Something moved in the trees. Not birds.*

I read this section a dozen times. Something changed here. From this point, Uncle Felix's sketches grew erratic. A kind of fevered obsession crept in. Felix's field drawings had become looser, darker, more abstract.

*Tuesday, 3<sup>rd</sup> of September – Saw it again today—not a dream. Slime trail 10 meters long. No known predator leaves a secretion this thick.*

*Reached cave near tangled tree roots. Discovered specimen. Juvenile. 1 meter long, a neonate, newly hatched.*

*A new genus. I call it Terralimax Vorax, which means Voracious Earth Slug. They're carnivorous. God help us.*

I noticed, from there, the journal became less structured. Felix's handwriting loosened, line weight increased—ink strokes become *frantic*. Drawings now included rough anatomical sketches: radula teeth with notes in the margin "like obsidian blades," and notations on mucus composition "possibly corrosive, acidic—tissue loss on contact?"

*Friday, 6$^{th}$ of September – It was then I resolved to take the young, hatchling slug home from the wild, in order to study its growth patterns in a controlled environment.*

*Chaska warned not to do this. He called the slug "kamári" again—not a word for an animal, but a curse. A bad spirit. I laughed at this. Silly tribal superstition.*

*I managed to smuggle the slug through airport security back home, without arousing suspicion of the international biosecurity people. I sedated the slug by chilling it, which forced it into a dormant state of hibernation. Placed inside a custom-built, foam-insulated cooler, labeled as: "Live Biological Samples—Do Not Open" and forged legitimate-looking scientific documentation to pass customs.*

*Monday, 16$^{th}$ of September – Back home, at the lakehouse in Willow's Hollow now. Slug feeding well. Chicken hearts, beef scraps, some venison. Prefers fresh meat. Growth rate astonishing—tripled in mass in 10 days. Eyespots adapting—may detect* *motion? It watches me now. It knows I'm watching too.*

*Sunday, 21ˢᵗ of September – I woke to the sound of scratching behind the walls. Thought it was rats. Checked containment chamber. Empty. Slime trail across floor... up wall... experiment compromised? It's in the walls now. Dear God. I can hear it moving. It's not—*

I notice the rest of the entry is illegible. The journal page is stained with a viscous, acidic substance that has partially eaten through the paper. Then…

The wall doesn't just crack—it *explodes*.

Plaster and ancient, moth-bitten wallpaper detonate into the parlour as something massive and wet hurls itself through Uncle Felix's Victorian drywall. I stagger back, almost tripping over a stool, and stare at the thing oozing its way into the room.

It's a slug.

But not the garden-variety kind you flick off your boot.

No—this thing is almost the size of a Volkswagen Beetle with a mouth like a circular saw. Its mucous trail is a sizzling, bubbling smear that hisses as it eats through the wood floor. I smell it before I feel it—acrid, chemical, like burning bleach and rot.

"Oh hell no," I yell.

It senses me. Its slimy stalks twitch, and then—*shloop*—it lunges.

I run.

Through the hallway, boots thudding against Uncle Felix's creaky floorboards, my breath sawing in and out of my throat. Behind me, I hear the wet slap of its body as it slides after me, sizzling slime smearing across priceless floor rugs and into the old kitchen.

I don't stop until I hit the tile. I whirl, reach out blindly, and grab the first thing I can find—a broom leaning against the wall. Classic. Useless.

I jab it at the slug's eyestalks as it squelches into the kitchen after me. It pulls back for a second, mucus bubbling where the handle touched its flesh. I swing again, too hard—crack!—I smash the overhead light fixture.

Glass rains down around me.

The floor is a mess of jagged shards, glittering under the flickering ceiling bulb. The slug halts. Its first tentacle slides forward, but the moment it hits the broken glass, it shrinks back with a shrill, slimy *hiss*. Acid splatters. The tiles blacken.

"Oh," I breathe. "You don't like glass."

It circles me slowly, trying to find a clean path. I pivot inside my accidental moat of jagged lightbulb bits, holding the stupid broom like it's a sword. The slug slithers closer to the far wall, trying to go *up*.

That's when I see it.

It's climbing.

It leaves a gleaming trail of corrosive goo as it pulls itself up the faded wallpaper. The air fills with a chemical tang as drops of its secretions hit the floor and sizzle.

It's *above* me.

I freeze.

Mouth dry. Heart rabbiting. I should run. I *can't*. If I step outside the glass, I'm dead.

Then—

"*BARK BARK BARK!!!*"

I whip around. There, bounding into the kitchen like a knight in slobbery armor, is Buster. His tail's wagging, and his ears are flapping like he's just been called in for dinner. My heart leaps. "Buster!"

He lunges forward and starts barking at the monster like he's been chasing it in his dreams for weeks. The slug hesitates. It curls back slightly, pulling one oozing eye down to examine this loud, furry threat.

Buster growls deep in his throat, hackles raised.

But the slug rallies. It lunges again—this time straight for both of us.

"MOVE!" I shout, grabbing Buster by the collar and yanking us both into the walk-in pantry. My back hits the shelves. Cans of beans and dusty spices rattle. There's nowhere to go.

It's coming.

Closer.

The air turns hot and wet with the stench of rot and acid. I hold Buster close, hand on his chest, his heartbeat pounding against mine.

This is it.

We're dead.

Unless—

My eyes land on something. A big, plastic tub wedged beneath the bottom shelf. The label is faded, but I know what it is. *Salt*. I kick the tub.

It wobbles.

I *kick it again*. Hard.

*CRASH.*

The lid pops off. Salt pours out like white gold, flooding the slug's path. It oozes right into it.

The effect is immediate.

The slug *screams*. Not with sound—but with motion. It rears back, its massive, slimy body convulsing. The salt sticks to its mucous membrane, and suddenly it's frothing—*boiling*. Blisters rise across its flesh. Its skin begins to *liquefy*.

Steam pours off of it.

It thrashes wildly, its own acid burning through the wooden floor beneath it. A hiss like a teakettle fills the pantry. Buster whimpers, and I hold him tight, both of us backed into the farthest corner.

The slug convulses one final time, lets out a long, bubbling *shriek*—and then melts into a heap of sizzling ooze and salt-foam.

Silence.

Only my breath. Only Buster's tail thudding weakly against the floor.

I wipe the sweat from my face with a shaking hand.

"Bad news, buddy," I murmur, "we're never eating escargot again."

Buster licks my cheek.

I laugh, a shaky, stupid laugh.

***

In the months that followed, I roped in Hector to sell the lakehouse. Eventually, some developer snapped it up. I hear they're planning to bulldoze the whole thing and start fresh.

Good. Let them.

A few weeks later, an article popped up in the local paper: "Novelist Battles Giant Slug in Lakehouse Horror." The headline goes viral.

I shelved the detective novel I'd been working on—turns out gritty crime just doesn't hit the same after you've fought off a carnivorous gastropod.

Instead, I wrote a horror novel. Total schlock. I called it *Moist*. It's about a giant slug that terrorizes holidaymakers in a creepy old lakehouse.

It became a bestseller!

Some folks from Hollywood rang. They want the film rights. Only issue—they hate the title. They want to call it *Slime*.

Whatever. It's their money.

Jane broke up with Wade (turns out "rich" doesn't always mean "interesting") and we found our way back to each other. We're figuring it out. Slowly. But it's real this time.

Buster gets his daily walks, extra treats, and now sleeps with one eye open. Just in case.

And me? I'm doing fine. Just don't ask me to go anywhere damp. Or show me another damn slug. Ever again.

# Chimera

"There's no one here, Lieutenant," Hobbs said, over the whir of the tank's engine, as they motored forward through the mud and the rain. "It's fuckin' crickets."

Lt. Miller scrutinised the crumpled map he'd taken from a dead Colonel, back in Břekov. He rubbed his beard. In the dim glow of the interior light his face was lined, his eyes like piss-holes in the snow. It had been thirteen days of fierce fighting, Operation Nightjar was a bust, and they needed to rejoin the 51st infantry.

"You sure we're not lost, El Tee?" Lipinski asked.

Miller frowned. "Aitch, pop up and take a look."

Hobbs opened a turret hatch and manned one of the mounted, M240 machine guns, training it on each building as they passed. His pulse quickened as he imagined being targeted by a sniper—it didn't help knowing the Balkovians were notoriously inaccurate.

The town, if you wanted to call it that, was a patchwork of ramshackle huts, with flat corrugated iron roofs, in the middle of butt-fuck nowhere. Hobbs scanned from side to side and noticed a plume of smoke billowing from a bombed-out truck. Beside it, in the long grass, lay the carcass of a dog. Caw, caw!—called a crow as it lit upon the corpse and pecked at its eyeball.

"Jesus, what a shithole," Hobbs said, over the intercom.

"We should have stayed in Břekov," Lips agreed.

"Save that chatter," Miller said and banged his palm on the driver's internal door hatch. "Take it slow. We don't want to frighten any civilians."

"Right, Lieutenant," Garcia said, decelerating. He sat forward in a separate driver's suite.

"Wait!" Hobbs said, and all sixty-eight tons of the tank's reinforced armour and steel shuddered to a stop. *Movement.* He switched to his field glasses. A lone woman approached from the end of the town square. She was tall and wan and walked with an unusual gait. "Is everything alright, Ma'am?"

Nothing. She gave no response.

Something was wrong—very wrong. Hobbs felt a familiar itch in his trigger finger. "We're peacekeepers," he said, trying again.

"What's the hold-up?" Miller said, emerging from the other hatch.

Hobbs pointed, just as a man shuffled from a nearby doorway and joined her. A third person, then several more appeared, forming a steadily amassing crowd.

"What's their malfunction?" Miller said, tilting his head. "STOP!" he yelled, the tendons visible in his neck. "GET ON THE GROUND, NOW!" But the crowd, by then a veritable horde, was unfazed by Miller's commands and kept up their steady approach.

"They're sick!" Hobbs cried, seeing the tumour-like growths on their skin.

A look of disgust crossed Miller's face, his jaw muscle twitching. "Pop that bitch."

Hobbs nodded and, reluctantly, fired a single burst of machine gun fire. It never was like the movies. The bullets struck the woman, tearing flesh from bone, leaving a gaping exit wound the size of a typewriter. She went down, shaking and spasming.

Oddly, the others in the crowd didn't react. There were no screams or running.

"Whoowee, you got her!" Lips said.

Moments later the woman stood, like some kind of unholy, Balkovian Lazarus, and resumed her shuffling, her intestines trailing from her torso.

"Oh shi-it!" Hobbs said, reeling back. The horde let out a collective moan, and an eerie, fire-like glow emitted from their mouths.

"Light 'em up!" a horrified Miller cried.

The two opened fire with the M240s, raking the crowd with a hail of 30mm armour-piercing rounds. The gun muzzles flashed, and the people fell, like so many wheat stalks for the reaping, the ground slick with their blood and viscera.

"Goddammit," Hobbs said, wide-eyed and panting when they finally stopped firing. All was still and the air was heavy with the sweet tang of gunsmoke. Before them lay a bloody carpet of broken and dismembered bodies.

There came a furtive and sibilant sound like a snake slithering across cobblestones. Hobbs watched in terror as the flesh and sinew of the dead rose in an undulant wave, merging and coalescing, shunting together into one near–amorphous mass. The result was an abhorrent creature with dozens of human legs and arms. These appendages lengthened and it began to walk on them like spider's legs.

"Fuck! Close your hatch," Miller exclaimed. Inside, they scrambled to their battle stations. "Back her up. Let's move!" he yelled at Garcia.

The tank's engine revved, and they moved rapidly backwards. The creature bounded after them, gaining momentum. Its elongated legs thundered on the stamping-ground, its multitudinous arms flailing. A single wide, grotesque mouth had formed and emitted an orange, fire-like glow.

"Load!" Miller said.

"Loading," Lips responded, working the foot lever to the ammo compartment, chock full of explosives, transferring a 120mm shell to the main gun.

Hobbs could hear the fear in the Lips' voice.

"Traverse right!" Miller called

"Traversing right," echoed Garcia, and the tank lurched, the left caterpillar track speeding up as the right slowed, facilitating the turn.

"I've got eyes on it," Hobbs said, aiming. There was a mechanised whir and the gun turret rotated. The creature had grown close to twelve feet high and still shambled towards them.

"Fire!" Miller called.

*BADOOM!*—came the resounding report of the main gun. An anti-armour piercing, super round hit the thing dead centre and it exploded, blood and flesh raining down everywhere.

***

"Can we talk about what happened back there?" Hobbs said as they made their way along the winding road, through the pinewoods behind the town. "I've seen some crazy shit before, but—"

"Don't ask, cos I don't know," Miller said. "Just be glad this turret is sealed. We'll report it to the top brass when we get back. Maybe they can explain what happened?"

Several klicks later they came across a compound with dilapidated, low-rise buildings, surrounded by a razor-wire fence. The facility was dark and intimidating and didn't match the surroundings.

"What's that sign say?" Miller asked.

Hobbs—who could speak a little Balkovian—"Army Medical Facility. Restricted area. No trespassing"

"What, like a hospital?" Lips said.

"I don't like it," Hobbs said. "Shouldn't we get back to base camp?"

"We have to seize every opportunity, private. We just got to hold it together and keep advancing," Miller said, ramming his fist into his palm. "Forward!"

The tank nudged the fence, knocking it down and flattening it beneath its treads. They drove through the compound, passing rows of grey, official-looking buildings, with mottled brickwork. It was late in the day and every arch, eave and mantle, cast an ominous shadow.

A moment later, an enormous aircraft hangar rose before them like an ancient monolith, a chilling citadel, obscuring the tree line and sky.

"Looks inviting?" Lips cracked.

"Dismount," Miller said. "We're gonna take a look. Garcia, stay with the tank."

The three men carried M9 pistols, including Hobbs who also had the M4 rifle.

Hobbs eyed the CCTV cameras. "There's big brother. Now, where are the guards? It's too quiet."

Lips inspected the door. "It needs a swipe card to get in."

"Can you override it?" asked Miller.

Lips took a card from his wallet, inserted it between the door and the doorframe, and gave it a jiggle. There was a metallic—click—and the door swung open. He laughed. "Bond. James Bond."

Inside, was a large demountable, with a series of connecting chambers. The crew ascended a set of stairs, passed through a door with a curtain of air, and found themselves in a darkened hallway.

Lips found the light switch, and they proceeded slowly down the hall until they came to a laboratory. The lab was equipped with a maze of computer consoles, suspended beakers, and test tubes. There were cages on either side filled with screaming animals: dogs, monkeys, cats, and rabbits. But what caught their attention most was an incubator, a glass cell with double-tempered security glass. Something shifted and slithered inside.

"What the fuck is that?" Hobbs said as a serpent-like creature pressed itself against the glass. It was a horrid mutation, with the head of an alligator but conjoined to a goat. The alligator's teeth gnashed while the goat's head lolled and let out a baleful bleating.

"Oh, God, I think I'm gonna puke," Lips said.

There was a stumbling sound. Hobbs went to investigate. A portly man in a lab coat sprang from under a desk. He tried to make a run for it but Hobbs collected him with the stock of his rifle and he went down like a sack of proverbial.

"Who the fuck are you?" Miller said, pointing his gun.

The man knelt with hands raised, blood trickling from his nose.

"You've made a mistake in coming here," he said, with a heavy Balkovian accent.

"Oh, and why's that?"

"Ver...iss...the gold?!" said Lips, in a hammy German accent."Tik tik tik, we have vays of making you tok."

"Gold? What gold?" the man said, quizzically.

"Lips, stop foolin' around and stand over there, you jackass," Miller said. "And don't touch anything." Lips shrugged and took position over by one of the consoles.

The man groaned, putting a palm to where Hobbs had hit him. "You're all fools. Don't you realise this facility has been compromised?"

"Compromised?" Hobbs said, furrowing his brow.

"A leak—a contagion," the man said. "Unlike anything the world has ever seen. I'm a scientist, the last surviving member of a team. We thought we were doing God's work." He laughed. "How wrong we were."

"What did you do?" Hobbs said, accusingly.

The scientist shrugged. "We've been splicing animal embryos for years—for medical reasons. Such hybrids are called chimeras."

"Kai-me-what?" Miller said.

The man shook his head. "Kai-meeuh- ruh, after the creature from Greek myth. A creature so ferocious that none could approach without being consumed by its flames."

"Cute," said Lips, lighting a cigarette.

"We called it the chimera virus. We thought we'd found a way to treat cancer. Only the virus changed, causing a rapid mutation in its subjects. It's essentially a contagious form of cancer: the tumour cells jump from the infected to the uninfected."

Hobbs exchanged a glance with Miller. "I think we just saw your handiwork back in town."

"Yes, very regrettable. I knew people there….but those townspeople, and these pets," referring to the goat-thing, "are nothing compared to what's stalks outside. The virus was weaponized for the war effort. A cybernetically enhanced organism was created, an amalgamation of multiple species—a killing machine."

"I call *bull-shit!*" Lips said.

The scientist shushed him. "Please be quiet."

"Or else what?" Lips said, brushing against the console controls. *WOOP, WOOP!*—an alarm began sirening, the monkeys began shrieking, and animal sounds erupted on all sides. Lips grimaced.

Miller stared daggers. "I swear to God, Lips," showing the back of his hand.

A blood-curdling and terrifying *ROAR* rose up from outside, deafening.

The scientist's eyes widened. "You've doomed us all."

"Back to the tank," Miller said.

"What about him?" Hobbs asked, referring to the scientist.

"Leave him," Miller spat.

"Took you long enough," Garcia said.

The sound of heavy, rhythmic footfalls—*BOOM. BOOM. BOOM*—approached, before the hangar was wrenched from its foundations. They heard the faint scream of the scientist, inside.

Garcia floored it just as the creature appeared. Hobbs' blood turned to icicles. It was the chimera, a cybernetic organism—part animal and part machine—just as the scientist had said. It had to be at least thirty feet tall and it moved like a panther. It lunged at them, roaring, its two gaping mouths, lined with conical, serrated teeth, emitting an orange fire-like glow.

"Incoming!" yelled Hobbs, as the creature unhinged its jaws, exhaling twin motes of fire. They felt the bone-jarring jolt as the flames hit the ground beside them.

"Steady now. Fire!" cried Miller, just as the tank completed a turn and the Chimera came into view. Hobbs's breath caught as he fired the main gun but missed.

"Don't fuckin' tickle it," Miller said. "Light that son of a bitch up."

"You ugly, mother—" Lips said, firing one of the side guns.

The creature flicked a telescoping, mechanical tail at them, tipped with three single-jointed pincers and they heard the—ping!—as it hit the side of the tank.

"Punch it!" Miller said, as they reached the edge of the compound. Garcia drove the tank through the wire fence at top speed, while the creature, still in pursuit, was gaining momentum.

"Reload!" Miller said.

"Got him in my sights," Hobbs said. The sound of the gun was deafening. The creature roared as the heated round hit its body, detonating. But, when the smoke cleared, the creature was unfazed and its skin was, already, rapidly healing.

"Fire at will!" Miller cried, as they raced across a grassy field, through a hedgerow, and up a steep incline. The chimera recoiled, readying itself for its next fiery breath. Thankfully, the rotation of the tank's gun turret was quicker. Hobbs fired. It was a hit. The creature roared in indignation.

"Brace yourselves," said Garcia, as they approached a deep, long trench—possibly, an old silage, forgotten by local farmers—running the length of the field.

"We aren't going to make it?" Lips yelled. The tank hit it at full speed, crossing the divide, but skidding to a sudden halt.

"The tracks are broke!" Garcia yelled.

"Fuck, fuck. We are so fucked," Lips said.

Miller and Lips popped up through the hatches and began firing the M240s. Bursts of machine gun fire rang out as they raked the stampeding chimera.

Hobbs could feel the colour drain from his face. They were sitting ducks. He fired with the main gun. It was a hit. The creature flailed about, and roared, but then breathed its awful fire weapon. Lips caught the worst of it and was grilled alive in the creature's heat beam.

"You, son-of-a-fucking-whore!" Miller cried, firing another salvo, but the chimera was too close, and he was covered with the creature's blood and ichor. He dropped down through the hatch into the turret.

"You okay?" Hobbs asked. Miller had gone pale and started convulsing and vomiting.

A moment later, Garcia emerged through the driver's hatch and started firing. Hobbs heard the creature's roar followed by screams. There was a sickening squelching sound, like the rending of human flesh, and Garcia fell silent.

Miller writhed in pain, his body twisting into transforming into unnatural shapes, his skin swelling and covered with tumours. An inhuman hiss issued from his mouth and he—or *it*—lunged for Hobbs.

Hobbs yelped in surprise and fired his M9, which started his ears ringing. He made a break for it, crawling through the forward hatch into the driver's compartment. "Get off me," he cried, as Miller grabbed hold of one of his boots. He kicked and managed to wriggle free, closing the hatch behind him—but not before tossing in a live grenade.

He made it out of the tank through the driver's hatch without the chimera noticing, and sprinted as fast as his legs would carry him, towards the trench, and dove in. He lay flat hunkering close to the earth. Seconds later there was a massive explosion as the grenade ignited the ammo compartment in the tank. Bright orange flames roared, spreading out in the air above him. The heat was intense.

After a while, Hobbs exited the trench, his ears still ringing, and surveyed the aftermath of the explosion. The chimera must have been blown sky-high. Bits of bone, meat, and flesh, littered the muddy ground. The wreckage of the tank sat in a crater, resembling a broken plaything, left behind by some thoughtless child. Black smoke and embers rose into a sunless sky.

# Fortune Bound

It was a warm October evening when the traveling carnival rolled into town. Jacarandas were in full bloom, their lavender petals glowing in the fading light, as a colony of fruit bats wheeled silently overhead. Shane walked hand-in-hand with his fiancée, Becca, weaving through the bustling crowd. Behind them, the great spokes of a ferris wheel stretched skyward, glinting like a web against the twilight. Nearby, a pack of children with painted faces ran skylarking between concession booths, balloons bobbing on strings behind them.

Shane never liked carnivals. He found them tacky and overrated—havens for misfits, and grifters. The rides bored him, the games felt rigged, and everything was overpriced. The whole scene seemed recycled, and overdone. He wouldn't have come at all if Becca hadn't talked him into it.

As they moved through the crowd, people bumped and jostled them, the grass underfoot worn to dirt by constant traffic. Hawkers barked from garishly lit stalls, carnies hustled their games with greasy smiles, all eager to part the crowd from their hard-earned cash.

After grabbing food, they passed an exhibition tent: *Lionel Spinx—The Human Skeleton* was mid-performance. Nearby, shrieks rang out from the dodgem cars, while strings of flashing bulbs lit up the night, casting the grounds in a jittery wash of color.

Spinx was unnaturally tall—nearly seven feet—and rail-thin, almost skeletal, just as his epithet promised. A contortionist by trade, he could twist and fold his body in ways that defied logic.

They watched as he slowly folded himself into a suitcase, every joint popping in protest.

"I think I'm going to be sick," Becca said, half-laughing, half-groaning. She grimaced, but the sparkle in her eyes gave her away—she was charmed more than repulsed. With her long, voluminous brown curls and striking eyes, she turned heads without trying.

Shane chuckled. "C'mon, let's go."

Not long after, they wandered down one of the back rows of the carnival, where the lights were low and the crowd thinned. Tucked away in a corner sat a weathered trailer. Down one side, in large, stylized copperplate letters read…

*MADAM ZARETA:*
*PSYCHIC,*
*MEDIUM,*
*CRYSTAL GAZING,*
*PALMISTRY,*
*NUMEROLOGY.*

"Oh, Shane, let's get our fortunes read. Come on, please?"

Shane rolled his eyes. He never put much stock in charlatans.

"Don't you want to know the future?" Becca asked, nudging his arm.

He sighed. "I'll come in if it matters that much to you."

It was a full-sized caravan, tacky and old. Inside, the dim lighting cast everything in a soft, amber gloom. The patterned wallpaper peeled at the corners, earthy tones dominated the small space. A dinette with a fold-out table sat between two upholstered benches, all cluttered with trinkets meant to suggest the mystical—hanging fabrics, flickering candles, a mosaic rug, and a fraying shawl tossed over a lamp.

Incense hung thick in the air. An oscillating fan buzzed quietly by the window, while tinny Eastern music played from a CD player in the corner.

Madame Zareta appeared from behind a beaded curtain. She looked to be in her seventies, dressed like a fortune-teller out of a storybook—headscarf, shawl, hoop earrings, and clattering bangles.

She welcomed them with a nod and gestured to the seats, speaking in a vaguely European accent. French? German? Shane couldn't tell.

Next came the part where she did her whole *"cross my palm with silver"* bit—only in this century, it meant Shane had to tap his MasterCard on a wireless reader.

Zareta had already arranged her props: a deck of tarot cards and a glowing crystal ball, the kind you only ever saw in movies. It shimmered under the lamplight, casting distorted reflections on the fold-out table.

"What question have you come here to ask?" she said, her voice smooth and rehearsed.

Becca glanced at Shane, then back to the fortune-teller. "I don't know... I guess... will I be happy, y'know, in the future?"

Madame Zareta slid a pair of half-moon glasses onto her nose and took Becca's hand gently in hers. "You can learn much from the lines of a hand," she said, studying the palm as if deciphering ancient script.

Becca shifted in her seat. Shane gave her other hand a quick, reassuring squeeze.

"This line here—your life line," Zareta said, tracing it slowly with a cool finger. "Long. Unbroken. That's good. It means you'll live a long, contented life."

Becca beamed. Encouraged, she asked more questions—about love, success, family. Zareta's answers were warm, vague, and just reassuring enough to feel personal. It was exactly the kind of soft certainty Becca seemed to crave.

By the end, she was smiling, joking, her earlier nerves gone.

Then Zareta turned to Shane.

The process began the same way.

Zareta asked, "What question did you come to ask?"

Shane shrugged. At a loss, he echoed Becca's earlier words: "Will I be happy?"

Zareta took his hand, studying the lines. Her brow furrowed. "Hmm. Interesting—pardon me," she said, releasing his hand. Then, without explanation, she reached for the crystal ball.

Becca raised an eyebrow.

Zareta stared into the iridescent orb, her gaze growing vacant, pupils dilating. Her body went still, trance-like.

Becca gave Shane a questioning look.

Zareta's face was stony, focused.

Shane wasn't impressed. He didn't buy the act—he knew the type. Psychics were hustlers, running a well-practiced con.

But then something shifted. The old woman jerked slightly, a strange expression flickering across her face—puzzlement, then… something else.

Flustered. Surprised.

"Excuse me," she said abruptly, stepping away from the table. At the sink, her hands trembled as she poured herself a glass of water.

"Are you okay?" Shane asked.

"Oh, fine," Zareta replied, waving it off. She returned to the table, attempting to resume the reading—but her voice lacked conviction.

Something was wrong.

Even Shane, the skeptic, began to wonder.

He stayed silent at first, but the question gnawed at him. Finally, it burst out:

"What happened? Did you see something? A vision?"

Zareta hesitated. "No, nothing like that," she said, swallowing.

Shane knew a lie when he saw one.

"No, really. What did you see?" He cleared his throat. "If it's something serious—an illness, an accident—I think I deserve to know."

Zareta's lips thinned. "I'm very sorry. I can't continue. I'm going to have to ask you to leave. I feel a migraine coming on."

"Horseshit," Shane snapped, rising to his feet.

"Shane!" Becca gasped, placing a calming hand on his arm.

"Just tell us what you saw," he said, voice hard.

Zareta glared. "I've had enough. Out. Now." She pointed to the door.

"But—"

"Out!" she shouted, ushering them out and slamming the trailer door shut.

Shane stood there, stunned. A heavy sense of dread crept over him, cold and unwelcome.

"She's crazy," Becca muttered, shaking her head. "C'mon. Let's go home."

***

"Days passed, but Shane couldn't stop wondering what the fortuneteller had seen in her crystal ball. What had she glimpsed? He was sure she hadn't told him everything. Her reaction—tense, almost fearful—suggested something awful.

246

*I'm spiraling. Obsessing.*

But how could he not?"

He'd been down in the dumps for days. Then, while absentmindedly flipping through a newspaper, something caught his eye—a psychic hotline ad. *Madame Zareta.*

He stared at the number. Could it really be her? Her *cell* number?

*I can just call her,* he thought. *Apologize. Maybe she'll understand. Maybe she'll finally tell me what she saw.*

With a flutter of nerves, he dialled. The phone rang a few times before a woman answered.

"Hello?"

"Madame Zareta?" he said quickly. "This is Shane Goodman. I don't know if you remember me— my girlfriend and I saw you last weekend for a reading? You had a migraine. There was... a misunderstanding, and I just wanted to apologize—"

A sharp inhale.

*Click.*

The line went dead.

He stared at the phone. "What the—?"

Why would she hang up?

A chill crept down his spine. Something wasn't right. *Was there something she saw in his fortune—something bad?*

He had to know.

***

The next day, during his lunch break, Shane returned to the carnival. He was determined to speak with Madame Zareta. He would apologize, try to appeal to her better nature. What was the big deal, anyway? Fortune-telling was just a load of nonsense. Mullarkey. But then again—what if it wasn't?

What if he *was* fated for an accident or illness? Could he really take that chance? He had to know what was in store for him.

As he stepped onto the field where the carnival was set up, he bought a ticket and pushed through the crowd, past the gaudy concession stands. The air was thick with the sugary scent of popcorn and roasted nuts, but now it turned his stomach. Laughter rang out—sharp, high-pitched—and to Shane, it sounded like mockery. Were they laughing *at* him?

*Stupid, Shane. How could you fall for that kind of quackery?*

Still, he couldn't ignore the nagging pull in his gut. He needed answers. He needed to know.

Up ahead, he spotted Madame Zareta adjusting the sandwich board outside her trailer. As soon as he saw her, he broke into a jog.

"Madame Zareta?" Shane called, breathless. "Can I speak with you?"

She glanced at him—and froze. Her eyes widened, the color drained from her face, and without a word, she turned and rushed toward her trailer.

*No,* Shane thought.

He chased after her and, desperate, slammed a hand against the trailer door just as she tried to pull it open.

"Go away," she snapped.

"Please—just talk to me. About my fortune. Why did you stop the reading? What did you see? I need to know."

"Leave me alone," she said, struggling to pry the door from his grip.

"Tell me! Why won't you talk to me?"

"You stay away from me, you hear?" she shouted, finally yanking the door free. She disappeared inside and slammed it shut with a thud that seemed to echo in his chest.

Shane stood there, stunned. He ran a hand through his hair, trying to make sense of it all. He was bewildered, frustrated—and no closer to the truth than before. What had she seen that frightened her so badly?

His fingers brushed against something in his pocket. The carnival ticket. A symbol of joy and escape. But today, it felt hollow.

He turned and walked away, the noise of the carnival fading behind him. There was no celebration in him now—only questions.

***

Afterwards, Shane made his way to the pub. He settled onto a stool, nursing beer after beer in lonely silence, trying to drown the weight pressing down on him. That's when he spotted someone familiar across the bar—none other than Lionel Spinx, the human skeleton.

"Hey, you're him, right?" Shane said, sliding onto the stool beside him.

"One and the same," Lionel replied with a grin, twisting his bony fingers into a quick, quirky contortion—a party trick that made Shane chuckle. "But around here, just call me Lionel."

Shane nodded and tapped the counter in front of him. "Same again for this man."

"Sa-ay. Thanks," Lionel said, flashing an impish smile.

Ten minutes later, they were deep in conversation, talking like old friends. Shane leaned in. "Do you know anything about Madame Zareta?"

"We go way back," Lionel said. "All the way to the start of the carnival. She's like a second mother to me."

"Do you know much about her? Like... where she's from? Is all that psychic stuff for real?"

Lionel laughed, taking a slow swig from his glass. "Her name? Just a stage name, same as mine. All smoke and mirrors. She's really Susan Billington from Calgary. That accent? Total act."

"Seriously?" Shane raised an eyebrow.

Lionel chuckled again. "But the psychic stuff? That's real. She's the genuine article, my friend."

He let out a tired sigh. "She even predicted what would happen to Old Gus."

"Who's Old Gus?" Shane asked.

"The strongman," Lionel said. "Used to be, anyway. Now he's a sideshow act—can't move without a wheelchair."

Shane frowned. "What happened?"

"Old Gus got addicted to the spotlight— always chasing a bigger stunt, heavier weights. He was billed as *The Strongest Man on Earth*, and he believed it a little too much. Arrogant. Reckless. Zareta warned him it would be his downfall. She told him exactly what would happen. But did he listen? Nah. He just laughed."

Lionel's voice darkened.

"It happened during a show. He was lifting a car—part of the act—but the rig failed. The whole mechanism backfired. The supports gave way, and the weight tore his arms right out of their sockets.

Almost killed him. Now he's dying slow... an inch at a time."

Shane's stomach turned. A chill crept up his spine. Maybe there *was* something to this fortune-telling stuff after all.

Lionel studied him. "Why the sudden interest?"

"No reason," Shane muttered, downing his drink and looking away.

***

The next morning, Shane sat at the kitchen table, stirring his coffee in slow circles, eyes fixed on his untouched breakfast. Becca was talking—something about plans, or maybe just filling the silence—but her words blurred into a low, monotonous hum that barely reached him.

She sighed, breaking the silence. "You've got to let this go, babe."

Shane looked up, blinking. "What?"

"You know what I mean," she said gently. "Nobody really knows what the future holds. Not for sure."

He stared into his cup. *Maybe fate is just a chain,* he thought. *And if I could find the weak link—press hard enough—I could break it. Get out.*

"But you do," he murmured, nodding toward her. "You had your fortune read."

Becca tilted her head, studying him. "I didn't think you bought into that stuff."

Shane gave a short, humorless laugh. "I don't."

She raised an eyebrow. "Right."

"It's just..." He trailed off.

"It's been days," she said, her voice firmer now. "You're stuck on this."

"I don't know if I *can* let it go."

Becca's expression tightened. "This isn't good for you, Shane. It's not healthy."

***

At work, Shane stared blankly at his computer screen, chin resting on his palm. His eyes drooped, and his head dipped slightly as he began to nod off.

"Am I interrupting?"

Shane snapped upright. His boss, Mr. Carver, approached. Tall and broad-shouldered, Carver wore a tailored navy suit and a steel-grey tie that matched his stern expression. A tablet was tucked under his arm, and his polished shoes made little sound on the carpeted floor of the trading office.

"Ah—no," Shane said quickly, straightening in his chair. He fumbled with his mouse. "I was just recalibrating the risk models for the emerging markets portfolio."

Carver raised an eyebrow but didn't comment. Instead, he cleared his throat.

"We've got a problem. You still haven't handed in the Volatility Impact Summary report."

Shane blinked. "I thought that wasn't due till Monday?"

"You didn't get the memo? The deadline was moved up."

"Jeez—really? Sorry, I must've missed that."

"Mm-hm. Well, if you could go ahead and get that finished ASAP, it would be appreciated."

Carver turned to leave, then hesitated.

"Oh, and Shane?"

Shane looked up again, a flicker of unease crossing his face.

"I stopped by your desk yesterday afternoon. You weren't here."

Shane's throat tightened. He gave a quick, too-casual shrug. "I must've been in the break room."

Carver didn't say anything at first. He simply stared at Shane, then slowly raised an eyebrow and gave a small, skeptical nod.

"Right. That report—today, please."

Without another word, Carver turned and walked off.

***

Shane knew he had to confront Zareta—or Susan Billington, or whatever her real name was—if he ever wanted closure. If there was any hope of returning to normal, he needed answers. He needed to know what was in store for him—his future. She might turn him away, sure. But this time, he wouldn't leave. He'd insist she finish what she started. He deserved the truth.

So, early one morning, he drove back to the carnival grounds.

But as he pulled up, he froze.

The lot was empty.

No flashing lights, no echo of music, no Ferris wheel towering above the treetops. Just silence.

*No... this can't be happening.*

He stepped out of the car and walked to the centre of the field. No concession stands. No dodgem cars. The long grass had been flattened in patches, and here and there, bits of popcorn boxes and trampled streamers lay abandoned in the dirt—ghosts of the carnival that had vanished overnight.

A cold wind stirred, and he pulled his jacket tighter. The sky overhead turned a dull, steel grey.

A piece of litter tumbled past—pirouetting on the breeze like a tired ballerina at the end of her routine. Shane bent down and picked it up.

It was a flyer.

*THE GRAND MIRAGGIO CARNIVAL*
*Now appearing in:*
*Geelong – 3 days*
*Lara – 2 days*
*Bacchus Marsh – 2 days*
*Next stop: Daylesford*

Shane's eyes locked onto the last town.
*That's only four hours from here.*
He pulled out his phone, called work, and feigned a sore throat. After hanging up, he drove home, threw a few things into a bag, and hit the road.
He wasn't letting this go. Not now.
He would follow the carnival—
And face the fortune-teller.

***

Shane checked into a seedy motel on the outskirts of Daylesford. The kind of place that reeked of mildew and decades of regret. The neon *VACANCY* sign buzzed and flickered like a dying insect above the cracked brickwork. The clientele were mostly teenage runaways or long-haul truckers trying to sleep off the road.

His phone buzzed again. Becca.

He let it go to voicemail.

He waited until nightfall, locked the flimsy motel door behind him, and drove to the carnival.

At the gates, he joined the line, trying to look like just another punter. Multi-coloured bulbs flashed garishly, spelling out *Grand Miraggio* in signage so loud it almost shouted. A motorized billboard arched over the entrance—a grotesque clown waved robotically, its massive teeth chomping open and shut, eager to devour the night.

He bought a bucket of popcorn, more camouflage than craving, and slipped into the swirling chaos of the fair.

When he reached the fortune-teller's trailer, it was dark. Locked. Empty.

She must've stepped out for dinner.

Glancing over his shoulder, he crept around the back. One window hung ajar. He peeled off the flyscreen, used a nearby cinderblock as a makeshift step, and hoisted himself through.

Inside, the trailer was steeped in darkness. The smell of patchouli, damp velvet, and a whisper of incense lingered in the air.

He crouched in darkness, breathing slowly, waiting.

*I will have it out with her,* he thought. *What does she know that she isn't telling me? I'll make her tell me.*

Time passed. Long enough that his legs cramped. Long enough for doubt to set in.

Then—a sound.

The rattle of a key. Metal in metal. The door cracked open, spilling a blade of pale light across the floor. A silhouette stepped in. He recognized the profile instantly.

Madame Zareta.

Or was it Susan Billington?

She hadn't turned on the light. Just stood there in the half-open door.

"Hello?" she called, voice uncertain. "Is someone there?

"You," she whispered, realization flickering across her lined face. Then she screamed.

He lunged forward, closing the distance before she could run. He grabbed her—not harshly, but firmly enough to stop her from bolting. This wasn't how he'd wanted things to go. He'd hoped it wouldn't come to this.

"Please," he said, pressing a finger gently to her lips. "I just need you to finish telling me the rest of my fortune."

But she didn't listen. She was in a frenzy, yelling, "Help! Murderer. Someone please help."

Shane panicked. Someone—carnies, passersby—might hear her screams and come running.

As he wrestled with her, trying to keep her restrained, his hand shot out toward a shawl draped over a lamp. He yanked it free and shoved it toward her mouth, desperate to silence her. But she spat it out, fury in her eyes, and started hitting him—wild, frantic blows.

One sharp elbow caught him in the nose. Pain burst through his face, his eyes instantly watering.

"Shut up, bitch," he said, feeling on the nearby table for something to tie her with. Instead, what he found was smooth and solid. In a panic, he picked it up and hit her with it.

A sound issued from her mouth, like— "Oof"— and she went limp, falling to the floor.

Shane was breathing heavy. *The bitch has a lot of fight in her.*

He found the lamp and switched it on.

Looking down, he realized what it was he was holding. It was Zareta's crystal ball—and it had blood on it. He'd made a mistake. He'd just meant to give the old girl a tap—something to shut her up, to knock her out—but he stove in her skull. Blood gushed from the wound onto the carpet.

"No, no, no. Shit!" he said, dropping the crystal. He looked around for the exit, but knew he couldn't simply flee the scene of a crime. There would be people, and soon police.

*Oh God. My life is over.*

She was still alive, but barely.

Her accusing eyes stared at him, one of her irises filling with blood. "Beast, murderer…" she whispered, her words garbled due to the injury.

Shane froze in place. In shock. *Oh God. I'm going to prison. I can't—I'm not cut out for that. I'm a desk job, morning-latte, never-even-had-a-speeding-ticket kind of guy. I'll get eaten alive in there with the murderers, the thieves, and the rapists…*

*What am I going to tell Becca? My life is over.*

He dragged a trembling hand through his hair, pacing, wild-eyed.

The shock of what he'd done curdled into annoyance—then boiled into fury.

"You stupid old witch!" he shouted. "Look what you made me do! You made me do this! I didn't want this!" He leaned in, put his hands around her throat, and began to strangle.

# Unfinished Business

"How was the date?" Maddie asked, brushing her hair over her shoulder. She was 23, beautiful, and unafraid to speak her own mind. She wore her usual blue hospital scrubs—standard attire for a medical clerk in the medical records department of Pineview Hospital.

"Nice," Kate said, taking a moment to consider. She envied Maddie's long, blonde hair, which seemed vibrant and gleaming compared to her own. She hesitated, not wanting to share too much—though they were friends, Maddie had a habit of letting things slip."

"Nope, you're not getting off that easy. I need details."

Kate sighed. "We saw a movie and fooled around. There's not much to tell, really."

"Fooled around, huh?" Maddie waggled her eyebrows.

"Stop," Kate said, giving her a playful shove.

The medical records room was typical of any hospital—pale walls, harsh fluorescent lighting. The space was arranged like a small reception area, with filing cabinets and shelves in the back. The hospital hadn't yet digitized all its records, so every patient had a physical file containing details of their condition, blood type, and prescriptions.

*WHOOSH*—an automatic door opened, and one of the doctors, an oncologist by the name of Jansen, approached. He was tall, balding, and kind of funny-looking.

"File that away, honey," he said to Kate, handing over some papers. His beeper chirped. He glanced at the message, then walked off without so much as a thank you.

The phone rang. Maddie answered.

*Line three. That could only mean one thing: a new admission to D Block.*

"Uh-huh—yes. We'll be up in a minute." She hung up and turned to Kate.

Maddie raised an eyebrow.

"Absolutely not," Kate said, bristling. "I did the last one."

Maddie pressed her palms together. "Pretty please? You know that place gives me the creeps."

Kate harrumphed. "Alright, but you owe me."

Grabbing a manila folder and a blank patient form, she made her way down the hall and took the elevator to the basement. Pineview Hospital sprawled like a maze, and reaching Block D from Block C meant navigating the underground corridor—a narrow passage lit by unforgiving fluorescent lights, stretching for hundreds of feet and skirting the edge of the hospital mortuary.

With the folder clutched tightly in one hand, she walked the corridor, the glare from overhead lights making her squint, gothic metal pounding in her earphones—a flimsy distraction from her mounting unease.

The hospital staff had, unofficially, nicknamed D Block *the farm*—as in *the funny farm*—for it was essentially the psychiatric ward. Kate hated to go there, especially at night. She could sense the negative energy of the place, the silent lamentations of the patients, their unhappiness pressing in like a weight.

She pushed through a set of double doors, and slipped off her earphones, as she approached a guarded nurses' station.

"Patient name?" asked the nurse at the front desk.

Kate gave the name that was given to them earlier.

The nurse busied herself looking through notes.

Inside the nurse's station was a bank of monitors, each showing black-and-white footage from the closed-circuit cameras installed in the patients' rooms. In the Farm, patients weren't allowed to roam freely—they posed a risk to themselves and others. At night, they were locked behind barred doors, and brought into the communal areas during the day, for meals and recreation. A patient could be seen, on one of the monitors, rocking back and forth, muttering, while another stood atop of their bed screaming at an invisible assailant.

"You can go through now," the nurse said, giving her the room number. There was a buzzing sound followed by a metallic—*click*—and the door unlocked.

A nurse was already in the room, checking the patient's vitals. No greetings were exchanged, so Kate quietly got to work, jotting down notes. As a medical records clerk, it was her responsibility to greet new admissions and ensure their files were in order.

The patient sat motionless, staring blankly at the wall. Their eyes were glassy, unfocused, a thin rivulet of drool tracing down their chin.

Kate left as soon as the examination was over.

As she briskly walked back through the underground corridor, music blaring in her earphones, she glanced at her phone—12:00 a.m. Midnight.

Overhead, the fluorescent lights buzzed and flickered.

Up ahead, a figure emerged from the shadows. *What the—? A patient?*

He looked like an old man—naked, crouched low, one hand pressed against the wall, feeling his way forward like he was blind.

She crept forward, hoping to slip past unnoticed. But as she drew near, the music in her earphones faded, replaced by a new sound—a harsh scrape of rough palms dragging along the wall.

*Don't look,* she told herself, edging past.

But curiosity won. She glanced sideways.

He was naked, pressed against the wall. Bald patches, raw and angry, mottled his scalp like a disease. He shifted just enough to catch her eye—a bloodshot sliver staring out from beneath a heavy brow.

A shiver crawled down Kate's spine. Something was wrong. Terribly wrong.

She quickened her steps—one, two—then he lunged.

Kate screamed and sprinted toward C Block, heart hammering.

Glancing back, she froze. The man was gone—vanished, as if he'd never been there at all.

***

"A ghost?" Maddie asked, raising an eyebrow.

Kate shot her a look. "I'm not sure what it was."

"What did it look like?"

"Like an old man," Kate said with a shrug. "Naked, with scabby bald patches all over his scalp. I figured it was just a patient who'd gotten loose from the farm."

Kate studied Maddie's face, catching the flicker in her eyes—doubt, barely masked.

"Well, I believe you," Maddie said, resting a hand on Kate's shoulder. "

Kate heard the words but sensed the lie underneath.

"What happened when you hit the alarm?" Maddie asked.

Kate inhaled sharply. "Security came running. They called a code blue."

Maddie frowned. "Code blue?"

"When a patient's out of bed and missing."

"Oh. Right, I knew that," Maddie said, trying to sound knowledgeable.

"They locked down the hospital and checked every bed while they searched for the missing patient."

"And did they find anyone?"

Kate shook her head. "No. Then they took me to the comms room to review the CCTV footage."

"We must've watched that same footage ten, maybe fifteen times," Kate said, fidgeting. "It was kind of fuzzy. You can see me walking across the corridor, the lights flicker, and then I do this weird dodge—like I'm avoiding something. I was freaked out. But there was no one else there. Just me."

Maddie frowned. "That's... weird."

"More like embarrassing," Kate muttered, burying her face in her hands. "The security guys looked at me like I belonged on the Farm."

"Are you sure about what you saw?" Maddie asked gently. "It was late. You were tired..."

"Why would I make something like this up?" Kate snapped.

"I told you—I believe you," Maddie said, but her voice lacked conviction.

Kate stared at her. "So what am I supposed to do?"

Maddie shrugged. "Maybe... just forget it happened?"

Kate dropped her gaze to the floor, her brow furrowed.

***

A week later, Kate was in the hospital cafeteria, lunch tray in hand, scanning the buffet line, when a chill swept over her, like someone had walked over her grave. In the plexiglass sneeze guard, she glimpsed a face—a stranger's—watching her.

She spun around.

No one was there.

Puzzled, she turned back—and froze.

Reflected in the glass was a ghastly face: pallid, half-wreathed in shadow and mist, its bloodshot eyes locked onto hers.

She screamed.

The tray slipped from her hands and crashed to the floor, her plate shattering on impact.

Around her, cafeteria staff stared in stunned silence.

"Kate, what's wrong?" Maddie asked, suddenly at her side.

Kate stood frozen, trembling. "Th-there—in the glass." She pointed with a shaking hand.

But the figure was gone.

Maddie followed her gaze, confused. Her expression softened when she saw the tears welling in Kate's eyes. Without a word, she pulled her into a hug.

Kate didn't resist. She melted into Maddie's arms, grateful for something solid, something real.

All around them, the murmurs and whispers in the cafeteria swelled, rising like static in the air.

***

Kate lived in a small studio apartment, just minutes from the hospital. It was afternoon. Her balcony door stood ajar, sheer curtains wafted in and out with the breeze. Wind chimes tinkled softly next door, while the distant cries of children echoed up from the pool in the complex, below.

Days had passed since the incident in the cafeteria, yet Kate remained on edge—nervous, unsettled, doing her best to hide it. She watered the potted fern on the windowsill, then settled on the couch to numbly watch a sitcom she wouldn't remember.

Her thoughts wandered back—again—to the figure she'd seen at work. It had terrified her. Her first brush with the supernatural, and it still didn't feel real. Was she losing her mind? Part of her wanted to quit the hospital, walk away, never look back. But another part—some strange, stubborn curiosity—kept asking questions.

*Who are you, old man? Why me?*

Later, in the bathroom, she undressed and peeled back the shower curtain. Stepping into the tub, she turned on the water and let it run over her. She closed her eyes—letting the warmth soothe her—working the shampoo into her scalp before rinsing.

When she opened her eyes, she froze.

Multiple strands of hair clung to her wet hands.

*No. Please, no.*

Her breath caught. Gingerly, she reached up and checked. Another clump came away in her fingers.

Kate whimpered—a raw, broken sound.

She slipped in her panic, grabbing at the curtain for support. The rod groaned, several rings snapping free. She staggered out, water dripping from her body, soaking the bath mat beneath her feet.

In front of the mirror, she stared at her reflection.

"No… no…" she whispered, fingers trembling as they traced the patch where her hair had come away.

And then—her reflection shifted.

Her skin sagged and puckered with wrinkles. Liver spots bloomed across her face. Her hair turned white, sparse, flaking from bleeding bald patches. It was him. The face she'd seen before.

He stared back at her through the glass.

Kate stumbled backward, a scream bursting from her throat. She clapped a hand over her mouth, chest heaving, heart crashing against her ribs. She felt herself unravelling—until the mirror began to fog over.

And then, in the condensation, a message began to appear—drawn by an invisible finger:

*HELP ME.*

***

Kate combed through the hospital records, hunting for any patient deaths that had occurred the previous Saturday. If her steady consumption of paranormal romance novels had taught her anything, it was this: spirits often linger where they die.

She scoured computer databases, flipped through endless paper files in the records room, and followed every lead. But in the end, her search turned up nothing.

With a frustrated sigh, Kate sank into a chair. Only one person had died that day—a young woman, a known drug addict who had overdosed.

Then a chilling thought struck her.

*What if he was never admitted as a patient at all?*

*Dead on arrival.*

*D.O.A.s went straight to the morgue.*

Kate hated the morgue even more than the farm—but she went anyway. She had to. Not just to satisfy her curiosity, but because she needed answers. She needed to know who the old man was and why he was haunting her.

Deep down, she knew it wouldn't stop. The ghost would keep coming—again and again—until she snapped completely. Maybe they'd lock her up in the Farm with the rest of the lost souls.

She jabbed the elevator button for the basement.

The morgue was ice-cold, thick with the sharp tang of chemicals and bleach. The air clung to her skin like plastic wrap.

"Whatchya doing here, Kate?" came a voice.

It was Clarence—the morgue tech. A tall, bull-shaped man, oddly wider at the waist than the shoulders, and always slightly out of breath.

"You're a long way from home," he added, sliding a cadaver tray into the cooler.

Kate offered a small, uneasy smile. "I know. I was hoping you could help me with something."

Clarence sniffed, then pulled out a crumpled handkerchief and blew his nose. "Really? My help? Sure, mi casa su casa. What's the problem?"

"I need to track down the name of a patient who may have died on their way to the hospital."

Clarence raised a brow. "Like a John Doe?"

"Sort of. Not exactly."

He scratched the back of his neck. "Lots of stiffs come through here. When was this?"

"Last Saturday."

Clarence rubbed at his stubbled chin. "Tall order."

"I know."

"Lucky for you,"—he tapped his temple—"I've got a memory like a steel trap. What did this guy look like?"

Kate described the old man, but when she got to the part about the bald patches in his hair, Clarence froze.

"What?" she asked.

"I remember that one," he said slowly. He crossed the room to a file cabinet, rummaging through a drawer. "Weird name, too. Something like... Adelstein? Applebaum? Ah—here it is. Amdursky. Harold Amdursky." He handed her the file. "Unusual case."

Kate tilted her head. "Unusual how?"

Clarence leaned against the counter. "When the paramedics got to him, he had severe abdominal pain—they thought it was a heart attack. But later, during the exam, we noticed something else."

Kate blinked. "What?"

"His hair was falling out. In patches. Diffuse alopecia. Not normal."

Kate's stomach knotted. "No, it's not."

"Right? Got some raised eyebrows, but management just chalked it up to old age and moved on. You know how it is."

She opened the file. The photo of Harold Amdursky stared up at her.

The hackles on her neck stood on end.

"You okay?" Clarence asked. "You look like you've seen a ghost."

Kate laughed nervously. "Can I ask you something? Even if it makes me sound completely nuts?"

"Now you've got me worried," Clarence said, frowning. "What's on your mind?"

Kate hesitated. "Do you believe in ghosts?"

He snorted. "Do you think I'd do this job if I believed in ghosts?"

She frowned.

"Kidding," he said with a grin. "Sure, I believe in ghosts. I also believe in UFOs, aliens, Bigfoot—the whole nine yards. Why?"

She pointed to the photo. "I've seen this man's ghost."

Clarence's face stiffened. "No shit? You're not messing with me?"

"No shit," Kate said. Then she told him everything.

When she finished, Clarence let out a long breath. "That's wild. What do you think he wants?"

"I don't know," she admitted. "I just need it to stop."

Clarence scratched his head. "If you go by the books—and all those cheesy ghost movies—he probably has unfinished business. Something is tying him here."

Kate thought it over. "So if I help him resolve it, he might move on?"

Clarence shrugged. "Did he have any family? They might know."

Kate scanned the file. "He had a daughter. Debbie Amdursky. She lives right here in Pineview."

Clarence gave her a look. "You're thinking of paying her a visit, aren't you?"

Kate nodded slowly. "I need to do something."

That evening, Kate searched the internet and found an obituary.

*Harold Arthur Amdursky 1ˢᵗ Feb 1944 – 9 December 2022, Aged 78*

*Much loved husband of Elizabeth who pre-deceased him in 2013. Wonderful father to Debbie. A Vietnam vet, lifetime model train enthusiast, and former president of the Pineview Model Railway Society. Cared for by his daughter, Debra, until he passed away from a heart attack at Pineview Hospital. He will be loved and missed by her and the wider community.*

***

The next day, she visited the address listed as Debra Amdursky's home. It was a misuse of hospital information—but she told herself the ends justified the means.

The house was a charming little bungalow nestled on a quiet, tree-lined street. A stately oak shaded the front yard, and manicured lawns framed the walkway. Yellow tulips bloomed in neat flowerbeds bordering the front patio.

Kate wrung her hands before raising one to knock. Footsteps sounded from within.

The door opened to reveal a tall, middle-aged woman who bore more than a passing resemblance to Harold—clearly a family connection. She wore a flour-dusted apron over a loose shirt and chinos, and the warm scent of something freshly baked drifted from inside.

"Yes?" the woman said, eyeing her curiously as she wiped her hands on her apron.

"Debbie Amdursky?" Kate asked.

"That's right."

"Hello, ma'am, I'm Tracey Allen," Kate said, inventing the name on the spot. "I'm a reporter with the *Pineview Times*. We're doing a piece on model train enthusiasts."

It was a complete fabrication, but it seemed preferable to the alternative: *Hello, I keep seeing the ghost of your dead father*—which would've landed her in a psych ward.

"I was hoping I could speak with you about your father, Harold Amdursky?"

"Oh my, this is quite unexpected," Debbie said, fussing with her hair.

Kate felt a pang of sympathy for the woman. She was clearly houseproud—probably a bit of a shut-in. *I bet she'd be thrilled to see her name in print,* Kate thought.

"Come in, then. You'll have to excuse the mess," Debbie said, leading her into the living room, which was spotless—almost unnaturally so. Debbie slipped off her apron and gestured toward the couch.

Kate caught a whiff of something sweet and buttery. "Mmm, what's that heavenly smell?"

"They're my madeleine cookies," Debbie said with a soft laugh. "I just put on a fresh batch."

"Well, they smell amazing," Kate said, pulling a notebook and pen from her bag, trying to stay in character. "Would you mind if I asked—what was your father like?"

Debbie tilted her head. "Gosh, where to begin? He was a good man, kind, hardworking. Always good to Mom and me. He worked for years at the North East Rail Corporation."

"Is that where he developed his love of model trains?"

"It was, although they forced him into retirement."

"Oh, that's sad."

Debbie hesitated. "Yes, it was—office politics. He was getting on in years, I guess... It wasn't until after he retired that he became president of the PHMRS."

"The PH…?" Kate scratched her head.

Debbie gave her a mildly suspicious look. "The Pineview Model Railway Society."

"Right, of course," Kate said quickly, covering. "He must have really loved model trains?"

"Oh yes. It was his only hobby." She paused, eyeing Kate with a mix of curiosity and calculation. Then, standing abruptly, she said, "Come. I have something to show you."

Kate followed her down the hall to the kitchen, where Debbie opened a narrow door.

"What's through there?" Kate asked.

They descended a set of creaky wooden steps into a dark, damp space below. The air was cool and slightly musty.

"Whoa," Kate muttered, nearly slipping.

Debbie tugged on a pull cord. A single hanging bulb flickered to life, flooding the basement with a warm, yellow light.

Kate gasped.

A massive model train set stretched across the room on a raised trestle table. It was a miniature replica of the entire town of Pineview—meticulously detailed, down to tiny houses, streetlights, and trees. Surrounding the table, shelves lined the walls, covered in dust and filled with mason jars of pickled vegetables. A pegboard behind an old workbench held neatly arranged tools.

"Aren't you going to take a picture?" Debbie asked.

"Huh?" Kate blinked.

"For the paper," Debbie added, raising an eyebrow.

"Oh, right," Kate said, forcing a smile. She pulled out her phone and snapped a few quick shots.

"You'll get a kick out of this," Debbie said, flipping a switch.

A soft whir came to life, and the miniature steam engine began to move—chugging and tooting as it looped through the tiny town.

"Woo-woo!" the whistle called.

Kate watched with amusement, but then jumped. Her heart lurched. In the shadows, something moved. A shape.

Harold's ghost stood there. Cadaverous. Wraith-like. Silent. Watching.

"Oops, scared you, did I?" Debbie laughed—a high, unnatural falsetto that reminded Kate of a hyena.

Kate forced herself to stay still, not wanting to react. Clearly, Debbie hadn't seen it. Evidently, the ghost was only visible to her.

Harold's pale, expressionless face remained fixed on her. Slowly, he raised one bony hand and pointed—toward the file cabinet against the far wall.

Kate swallowed hard. *What? What are you trying to tell me?*

Debbie's voice cut back in, oblivious.

"I've been meaning to clear out this junk. Might be something useful for your paper. But honestly, after all these years, I just want it gone." She gave a weary sigh. "If I ever find the time—or the energy."

Kate looked back.

The ghost was gone.

"You're not really a reporter, are you?" Debbie said once they'd returned upstairs.

Kate grimaced, still rattled from seeing Harold's ghost. "Is it that obvious?"

She hesitated, then sighed. "I work at the hospital. I'm not here on assignment—I just… I needed answers."

And so she told her everything.

To Kate's surprise, Debbie took it all in stride—no panic, no disbelief. She just listened, nodding calmly. Almost *too* calmly.

"Do you remember anything unusual about your father's death?" Kate asked. "Anything that might suggest he had… unfinished business?"

Debbie tilted her head, thoughtful. "Not really. Nothing comes to mind." She smiled, bright and easy. "Say, where are my manners? Would you like some tea? And you can try some of my madeleine cookies."

Kate hesitated. Then nodded.

Debbie returned a moment later with a tray—two steaming cups and a neat stack of shell-shaped cookies dusted with sugar.

Kate took a sip of tea, then nibbled a cookie. The flavor was delicate—lemony, buttery, almost too perfect.

"Well?" Debbie asked, watching her closely.

"They're lovely," Kate said.

"I'm so glad. It's an old family recipe," Debbie said with a nostalgic smile. "Notoriously tricky. You have to butter the pans just right, and the oven temperature—*very* precise. Otherwise, they collapse."

Kate blinked. Her vision wavered, blurring at the edges. The room swam slightly.

Debbie's voice drifted in, muffled, as though from underwater. "It's all about timing, really…"

The teacup slipped from Kate's hands and shattered on the floor. Pain stabbed through her abdomen, sharp and sudden. She gasped. The room tilted.

Debbie just stood there, smiling faintly.

Kate's knees gave out. She fell, the world tipping sideways—

—then everything went dark.

***

Kate awoke some time later, her stomach churning and sharp pains stabbing through her abdomen.

*Oh God. What was in that tea?*

She dry-heaved.

*Where am I?*

The room was dim, almost pitch black. She couldn't move. The distant whir of a model train looped endlessly in the background.

*Debbie Amdursky's basement.*

A tugging sensation. A shadow loomed above her, rifling through her pockets.

"Well, Tracey," came Debbie's voice. "Seems you're not a reporter... and your name isn't Tracey either, is it?"

She held up Kate's wallet and cell phone.

"You're just a little liar, huh? Couldn't help but snoop around?" She tutted and placed the items on a nearby table.

"What are you gonna do?" Kate slurred. Her words spilled together, heavy with nausea and dread.

Every nerve in her body screamed. Her mind had gone full DEFCON ONE.

Debbie turned to a pegboard mounted with tools. She plucked down a hacksaw and tested the blade against her thumb.

"I'm going to make sure no one ever finds you," she said with a breezy shrug. "Well, not all in one piece." She let out a high-pitched falsetto laugh.

Kate's stomach flipped.

*How did I not see it? She's completely unhinged.*

Debbie grabbed a garbage bag, stretched it open—and it tore. "Ugh, this won't do. I'll be back in a jiffy," she said, heading upstairs.

Inside her head, Kate was screaming: *I'm going to die. Oh my God. This bitch is going to kill me.*

From above came the sound of cupboards slamming, floorboards creaking.

Her eyes darted across the basement, searching. Her phone was out of reach. She could barely move. But then, she realized what she was leaning against.

*The file cabinet.*

Harold—the ghost—had shown it to her for a reason.

*What were you trying to tell me, old man?*

She tried to sit up. Agony ripped through her abdomen.

*Why can't I feel my legs?*

She wiggled her toes—they moved. Barely.

Gritting her teeth, she dragged herself upright and leaned heavily on the cabinet.

Creaks overhead.

*No, no, no. She's coming back.*

Kate yanked the cabinet drawer open.

Inside: a handgun. Black. Sleek. Serrated slide. Wooden grips.

*Thank you, Harold.*

She didn't know what kind it was, if it was loaded, or if it would even fire. But she grabbed it.

"What are you doing?!" Debbie's voice rang out from the top of the stairs.

*Please. Oh, please.* Kate raised the gun, hands trembling.

"Put that down!" Debbie was halfway down the steps.

The gun felt like it weighed ten pounds. Kate squeezed the trigger.

*BANG!*

The shot echoed like a thunderclap. Her ears rang. Her whole body recoiled.

Debbie's eyes widened. She clutched her stomach, bounced off the wall, and tumbled down the stairs.

She landed in a crumpled heap at the bottom.

"You... bitch," Kate slurred, limping toward her.

She nudged the body with the muzzle. No movement.

Dead.

In the ambulance, fading in and out of consciousness, Kate thought she saw Harold Amdursky's face above her—a pale, gentle face watching over her as the paramedics worked.

***

Later, at the hospital…

"They found a box of rat poison," Maddie said, "with crushed-up sedatives beside the kettle."

Kate's mouth was dry. "W-why?"

"You're lucky they got to you in time," Maddie continued. "Unlike her father. She'd been poisoning Harold for months—small doses. Stuff makes your hair fall out."

Kate stared at the ceiling.

Maddie shrugged. "The cops think she got tired of taking care of him. Maybe she figured she'd cash in early on her inheritance. She thought you were onto her, so she gave you a lethal dose of the same."

# ABOUT THE AUTHOR

Brent McGregor is the writer of over three books, including *Blood Tide*, *Strange Murmurings*, and *Denizens of Darkhaven*. He is a prizewinning author of horror and dark fiction, a member of the AHWA, and lives in Sydney with his wife, daughter, and dogs. His work has appeared in the Australasian Horror Writers' Association publication, *Midnight Echo*. And he is the winner of the 2024 Asylumfest Mayday Hills Ghost Story Competition. Brent likes to delve into the world of the terrifying by writing stories that combine both the weird and the uncanny.

Visit him online at BrentMcGregor.com and join his newsletter, or follow him on Instagram or Facebook.

# ACKNOWLEDGEMENTS

The stories in this collection represent a significant portion of my creative work between 2020 and 2025. None of this would have been possible without my wife, Amy. She is patient and understanding, a wonderful mother, and quite honestly the best person I know. Thank you, darling, for your incredible heart and invaluable support.

I would like to thank my daughter, Roxanne, for her boundless energy and infectious spirit. You bring so much joy to our lives.

I would also like to thank my parents, Stephen and Glynne, for their love, support, and guidance.

A very special thank you to my writing group and critique partners, the NightQuills (Jeff Clulow, Alister Hodge, Georgina Ballantine, and David-Jack Fletcher), who have been instrumental in helping me to reach this point.